STRANGER IN THE HALL

STRANGER IN THE HALL

TED RAMSEY

Ramshorn

First published 1988 by Ramshorn Publications
64 Hermiston Road, Springboig, Glasgow G32

ISBN 0 9510646 1 4

Cover design by Gillian Waugh, **art dept.**
Typeset by Waverley Graphics Ltd.,
6 Canongate Venture, New Street, Edinburgh
and Printed by The Print House,
2D West Telferton, Portobello Ind. Estate, Edinburgh

CHAPTER 1

Oscar Slater arrived in Glasgow by the London train on October 29, 1908. By Glasgow standards he was not a small man, five foot eight or nine (1·73m), well built, dark haired and sporting a luxurient, black moustache. His slightly olive skin and heavy accent marked him down immediately as being of foreign birth and upbringing. He was well dressed and with the amount of luggage that accompanied him he could easily pass as a successful business or professional man. On his arrival that afternoon he booked into the Central Station Hotel under the name of Adolph Anderson, giving as his former address, London, and his profession as dentist. There was nothing in either his appearance or behaviour to suggest that his arrival marked the beginning of the first act of a drama that was to echo down through the years.

Slater had been born in the small town of Oppelin, near Beuthen, 1869, in what at that time was part of Prussia and which is now part of Poland. The area was then, and still is, a centre for coal mining and heavy chemicals and hardly famed for its scenic beauty. Oscar Slater was not his true name, he had been born Oscar Joseph Leschzier of jewish parents. His father was a baker. At the age of eighteen, 1887, he not surprisingly left home for the bright lights and better prospects of Hamburg where he was employed as a clerk in a shipping company. At that time, however, there was conscription in Germany and when Oscar received the call he did what many others had done before him, he left Germany for France.

His two years as a clerk in Hamburg had convinced him that a lifetime in an office was not for him, he wanted a life where he was free to move when and where his fancy took him and where quickness of wit rather than punctuality was what mattered. In Paris he took up dealing in jewellery and, I fear, also the dealing in human flesh as a pimp.

At sometime around the turn of the century Slater came to Scotland for he was known to be in Edinburgh in 1900 and where he was using the name of Smitz. He was arrested under that name in 1901 in Edinburgh on a charge of assault. It seems that Slater was acting as a pimp for a prostitute when he got caught up in a fight with a customer. The customer pressed charges but when he found out that he would be required to appear as a witness he let the matter drop. Slater walked free but the incident had brought him to the attention of the police and his name went on to their list. Later that year, July 12, Slater was in Glasgow where at the Ibrox Registry Office he went through a form of marriage with a girl called Mary Curtis Pryor. From this marriage there was later a son.

The marriage, however, was not destined to last for in 1905 Slater was living in Brussels with a French prostitute called Andree Juino Antoine. Slater had seemingly met Andree originally in London and the couple had fled to Brussels to avoid Mrs Slater who was in hot pursuit. The lady did in fact catch up with them in Belgium and as a consequence the couple fled to America. This first stay in America was of short duration for within a few months they had returned and split up. Andree returning to Paris while Slater came back to Glasgow.

Contrary to what many imagine there is occasionally a real bond between a prostitute and her pimp and this seems to have been so in the relationship between Andree and Slater for almost as quick as they had parted they were back together again and once more in America.

This time the stay in America was much longer and Slater formed a partnership with a gentleman called Devoto, the pair ran gambling clubs in New York and Chicago over the next couple of years. Presumable Andree was also part of the entertainment for she was not the sort of girl to stay at home. The business seems to have been successful financially for when Slater left to return to England at the beginning of 1908 he left behind him a bank account with some $7,000 to his credit. Why they decided to return is unknown but it might well have been that they had attracted the attention of the local police, a natural hazard in their line of business. What ever the cause the couple returned to London where Andree established herself once more in her regular line of business while Slater carried on with some diamond dealing on the side. They were, however, not to be left in peace for Mrs Slater somchow got wind of their presence and once more she was in hot pursuit. It looks as though Oscar very cleverly, in an attempt to avoid his wife, did what was least expected of him, he came back to Glasgow.

For the first few days following his return Oscar spent his time renewing old acquaintanceships and establishing new ones. He also got some visiting cards printed in the name of Adolph Anderson, listing once more his profession as dentist. On November 4 he was joined by Andree and her maid. Catherine Schmalz, and the Central Hotel became too expensive. On the 4th he moved himself, Andree and Catherine into a boarding-house in Renfrew Street, passing off Andree as his wife. I doubt whether Oscar would have been interested but he was now staying next door to the scene of another famous murder that had taken place half a century before.

The boarding-house, however, was only temporary and Oscar set-to to find more permanent accommodation and the way in which he went about this task clearly shows that he had all the skills of the successful con-man.

Isaac Paradise was the manager of Stuart & Stuart, house furnishers, at 65 St Georges Road, near Charing Cross. The shop is still there and still carrying on its original business. On November 4 Slater called at the shop to enquire about their hire-purchase terms and while there he asked about a flat above the shop which seemed to be vacant. Isaac, never one to lose a customer, volunteered immediately to phone the house factor in order to find out the terms of rental. Thus when later Slater called at the factor's office John Marr, the factor, was already fairly easy in his mind as to the suitability of his prospective tenant.

The flat was on the second floor and consisted of four rooms, a kitchen and bathroom. As was common in such flats the kitchen had a recess for the servant's bed. The terms of rental reflected the current economic conditions. 1908 had been a year of slump and a lot of property in the city was standing empty but the signs were that trade was on the upturn. Pending satisfactory references Slater could have the flat on an initial eighteen months lease at an annual rent of £48. Marr raised no objections to the house also being used for the carrying on of the practice of dentistry.

Slater provided two names of previous landlords in London as his references and he wrote their names on the back of one of his visiting cards. It is amazing how impressive a little bit of cardboard can be. Within three days the factor had received an answer to his enquiries and as they were perfectly satisfactory Slater and his menage moved into their flat.

Slater also placed an order with Stuart & Stuart for furniture to the value of £170, £10 deposit and £4 per month thereafter. The furniture purchased was merely to furnish the sitting-room and one bed-room. Only the comforts of Miss Antoine's clients were clearly being considered for the rest of the house was furnished second-hand at the cost of a few shillings. It is interesting to speculate whether there was already another lady of easy virtue in residence in the close. One of the other householders was a Mrs Bernstein who seems to have been on friendly terms with the police.

Life at 69 St Georges Road quickly settle down to a pattern. By the nature of the business the household tended to sleep late and the occupants seldom ventured out before lunch. The evening meal was generally served at around seven o'clock after which Slater would sally forth going mainly to the Sloper Club, a gambling club of which he became a member. Andree would leave shortly after, heading for the bars of the music-halls where she would pick up her customers. According to those who knew her she was a tall, slender, good-looking girl who dressed elegantly. She was no street walker, she concentrated on the upper end of the market contenting herself with one customer a night. Possibly if she picked up two gentlemen the maid would assist.

Like all new tenants moving into a house certain small, necessary items had to be purchased and one such essential item was a hammer for breaking up coal. Thus one of the first purchases Slater made was a hammer and his choice speaks volumes for the man.

On November 10 Slater called at the hardware shop of Hepburn and Marshall of Charing Cross to buy a coal hammer and the one he selected was part of a card containing six handy household tools. The set consisted of a hammer, pliers, screw-driver etc., and cost 2/6d for the card, which is 12p in modern money. But even in anybody's money a set of tools which only costs coppers are almost certainly rubbish and totally unfit for any realistic purpose. The hammer might have been good enough to drive in the odd tack but as a tool to be subjected to constant use it could only have been a waste of money. Certainly at its weight, it weighed 8ozs (200grms), it was useless for breaking coal. What the purchase does reveal is that Slater had absolutely no idea as to what was required to break coal or anything else for that matter.

As a dealer in jewellery Slater generally had in his possession some quite expensive pieces, certainly expensive enough to tempt the attention of the thief and the mugger. For security he could have used the facilities offered by the banks but banks have notoriously bad hours and are quite unsuitable for a man who is doing most of his business outside of the normal banking hours. As a consequence he preferred to use the more convenient pawnshop. It was alleged at the trial that Slater was a dealer in stolen jewellery although there was no evidence ever presented to support this. Nevertheless I am inclined to believe that this was indeed the case for his method of selling—to individuals for cash in pubs and gambling clubs—lent itself to the moving of stolen goods.

When Slater arrived in Glasgow he had a number of items of jewellery in his stock. He had for instance, as well as the soon to be famous gold cresent brooch with its three rows of diamonds, a gold purse, three pearl studs, a diamond pin, a ring &c. In cash he had excess of £100. Within a few days of his arrival Slater had pawned some of the jewellery, not for any want of money but merely to have them kept in a safe place. The cash he received from pawning he divided between Government Stocks and the Post Office Savings Bank. He also had his $7,000 on deposit in an American Bank. All in all if he had realised on his assets he would have been worth some £1,700.

Much has been made of Slater's connection with gambling and it has to be admitted that he did spend a great deal of his time in clubs given over to that activity. But whether he was a gambler in the sense of one who plays constistently for high stakes is open to question. Much was to be made later of his alleged losses at the table but significantly no one ever quantified the losses nor did anyone ever come forward to admit to having become wealthy from his bad luck. My own opinion is that he probably gambled very little and that he used the clubs merely because they brought him into contact with the kind of people that he and his mistress might be able to do business with. There is some evidence to suggest that Slater did in fact take home men from the club and it is reasonable to suppose that they were not being invited just for a cup of tea.

CHAPTER 2

Marion Gilchrist was 84 years of age and she had lived for most, if not all, of her life in Glasgow. Born in 1824 her life spanned the era from the stage-coach to the aeroplane and she had been a witness to the rise of the city to become one of the main centres of engineering and manufacture in the world. Her father had been a successful civil engineer and when he died he had been able to leave his daughter, who had never married, well provided for. Like most Victorian families the family had been a large one and they must have been physically tough for they all lived well into old age.

The family home, at least in the latter years of the father, had been a rented flat at 15 Queen's Terrace, or as it was alternately known, West Princes Street. The area was not all that large (see map), bounded west and east by St George Road and the river Kelvin and north and south by Great Western Road and Woodlands Road. The long east-west axis was approximately one mile, the shorter axis being about a quarter of a mile. Originally the housing had been developed from about 1850 onwards for the better-off, it was only fifteen minutes walk from the business centre, but development had been piecemeal. As the city's transport expanded the middle-class had moved ever further from the centre and by 1908 the district had become middle and working class. Having lived in her flat for more than thirty years Miss Gilchrist was one of the oldest residents in the district.

The flat occupied by Miss Gilchrist (see plan) was a large one, it consisted of six rooms with a large kitchen and bathroom grouped around three sides of a large hall or lobby measuring eighteen feet by ten feet. The flat was the middle flat of a three storied building and entry to the top and middle floor flat was by a close. The bottom flat had its own entry direct on to the street. Unlike most Glasgow closes No. 15 had a door to the close fitted with a lock so that without a key any caller would have to wait for the close door to be opened. To save the tenants the bother of having to go down the stair to greet every caller there was a handle inside the flat which operated the lock to the close door. In the winter of 1908 the top flat was unoccupied so that the middle flat was enjoying sole use of the close.

As you would expect with one so old Miss Gilchrist tended to lead a quiet life with few visitors. In 1908 she had at least one brother and two sisters still living and of course she had innumerable nephews and nieces but as they too had other family visits to make then there was little time to visit Miss Gilchrist. Like many elderly ladies who never married and had no immediate family in her later life she had to pay the price for her earlier freedom. She did have one niece, Margaret Birrell, who lived only a few minutes away but the relationship was a strained one. Margaret had turned part of her flat into a massage parlour and the idea of her niece being involved in business might not have appealed to the old lady. Margaret, who at this time was 45 years of age, also had a male lodger who was 36. Whether there was anything indelicate in this relationship is not for us to speculate about but it was the kind of thing which gave rise to talk. It would be understandable then if the old lady found the whole thing embarrassing.

If Miss Gilchrist had few female visitors then she had even fewer male visitors. The doctor called regularly once a week to keep a general eye on his elderly patient but Miss Gilchrist was remarkably fit for her years. Nevertheless, being a good doctor he recognised that health was no bar to the prescribing of medication, more especially as prescribing increased the fee. But I have little doubt that the old lady enjoyed the weekly visits of the doctor.

Another regular visitor was Mr Robertson, her stockbroker, who called every Saturday afternoon. As much of her money was tied up in safe investments then there was little movement in the stock so that Robertson's visits were more social than business. Miss

Gilchrist relied heavily on her financial friend for general advice and he probably knew more about her private life than any other. All her other male visitors were men who called in their professional capacity such as the regular visit of the man who came to clean her jewellery.

Naturally with only one other person in the house, the maid, many of the rooms were unused. The bedroom next to the bathroom was used as Miss Gilchrist's bedroom while another bedroom further down the lobby was used as a kind of dressing-room. There was a large room at the far end with another smaller room leading off and normally this was referred to as the sitting or drawing-room but they were both unused. Instead Miss Gilchrist used what was usually described as the dining-room, it was the room adjacent to the kitchen, as a combined sitting and dining-room. The whole flat was expensively and tastefully furnished, much of the furniture being antique. Someone in the family seems to have been a collector for there was hardly an inch of wall which was not used to support a painting.

Miss Gilchrist enjoyed going out and every Sunday, attended by her maid, she was a regular worshiper at the nearby church, usually in the morning. She also made a point of personally paying all her bills and she used the occasions to whip the trades-people back into line when necessary. Nor was she put off by her years from making fairly long journeys and staying overnight.

Miss Gilchrist lived alone except for her maid and over the years she had had a number who generally remained with her until they married. She was by all accounts a good employer. In 1908 the current holder of the position was Helen Lambie, a young woman of 21 years. Unfortunately we know very little about Helen's earlier life but the life of one maid generally differed little from the lives of all the thousands of other young girls in service at that time. For this reason, in order to give the reader some idea of what life was like in service before the first world war, I have decided to give a brief description of my mother's experience who was some ten years Helen's junior and who came from a similar background.

Like Helen my mother, Ann, was brought up in a mining village, Standburn, near Linlithgow, and at the age of thirteen she was put out to service. Because of her tender years she was first placed in the services of a nearby farmer where presumably my grandmother could keep an eye on her. At fourteen she was sent to Edinburgh, where the money was better, to work as a ward-maid in the Royal Infirmary.

Although her life there to us might well seem to have been a form of slavery I never heard my mother speak of that period without affection and pride. The work was hard, my mother started at six in the morning and worked on with only short breaks for meals until eight o'clock in the evening. Life was just one continuous round of scrubbing and polishing from morning till night.

But there were compensations. Most of the maids tended to come from if not the same district then at least from the same background and so they were never completely among strangers. The maids slept in a long dormitory above the nurse's quarters so that there was plenty of companionship. In a way it was a bit like a girl's school. Time off was regular, one half day per week and permission to attend a place of worship of choice every second Sunday. For those who were interested there was always the opportunity for watching the nurses at work and after a while some of the maids became quite knowledgeable, certainly they knew as much about nursing as the first year probationer. My mother's unofficial training stood her in good stead some years later when a sawyer she was working with sliced off his thumb.

The turn-over in the hospitals was quite rapid and by the age of sixteen most of the girls had moved on to better paid jobs. In my mother's case she became a room-maid for a while in one of the large hotels in Edinburgh. She only ventured once into private service when she took a position with a Morningside family. This family consisted of the husband, wife and two daughters and my mother was expected to tend to all of their needs. Her day started at six in the morning when she was required to clean and set two fires, clean and prepare the dining-room for breakfast, brush all shoes, serve early morning tea and cook the breakfast. Only then was she permitted to break her own fast. The rest of the day was spent cleaning, scrubbing, washing and ironing and of course cooking until late at night. My mother only stuck the job for a few days, she rose early one morning and left without even saying goodbye.

It is not without significance that her next job was filling shells with explosives in a munitions factory which also entailed walking four miles along country roads in order to start at six o'clock in the morning. My mother thought it was a very good job indeed, and this after an explosion had taken place.

By 1908 Helen had worked for Miss Gilchrist for just over three years. Her previous employer had been Margaret Birrell and why Helen had switched to the aunt is unknown but no doubt Margaret reckoned that her aunt had poached her maid. Certainly as jobs in private service went, working for Miss Gilchrist was a fairly easy number. True the flat was large but Helen was young and healthy and she had only one mistress to contend with. Certainly all the visitors who later spoke about it declared that the house was always spotless and that in her attention to her mistress the maid could not be faulted.

But because of the circumstances Helen, in fact, was required to perform duties generally outwith her job description. For instance when the doctor called Helen was always present and it was with her that the doctor would exchange a few words on his way to the door. The doctor treated Helen not as a maid but as a nurse and indeed on the few occasions that Miss Gilchrist was unwell the doctor was openly full of praise for the care and attention his patient received at her hands.

Mr Robertson also thought highly of Helen as a

companion to his elderly friend. On one occasion when Miss Gilchrist had considered dismissing Helen he had spoke up in the maid's favour. What had happened was that Miss Gilchrist had discovered that some of her jewellery had gone missing and the only person who could have taken it was Helen. Robertson had advised caution saying that it was probably more a case of borrowing rather than theft and he offered to have a word with Helen about the matter. It would seem that Robertson had been right for when he next called Miss Gilchrist had told him that the missing jewels had re-appeared. Miss Gilchrist never mentioned the incident to Helen but from then on she had always kept the key to the wardrobe where the jewels were kept in her constant possession.

Mr Robertson was also convinced that Helen, who did most of the shopping, was fiddling the household accounts. However, he was also of the opinion that the sums involved never amounted to much more than a few coppers per week and so he kept his suspicions to himself. Interestingly enough he justified his silence on the grounds that as Helen was being called upon to perform extra duties without being recompensed then she had some justification for her fiddling. He reckoned that the cost to Miss Gilchrist of employing a proper companion would have been infinitely more expensive.

CHAPTER 3

The pawnshop is an ancient and honourable institution preceeding by many centuries the more upmarket banks. Under the sign of the three brass balls the ordinary citizen can obtain a prompt and easy loan of money against the collateral of personal possessions. The business is one of the oldest regulated businesses in Britain for since the days of Henry VII no pawn-broker has been able to carry on business other than by licence.

The customer needing ready cash takes his goods to the pawn-broker who values them and makes an offer as to what he is prepared to advance. As a rough guide the value is always approximately one quarter of the value of similar goods being sold as new. There is no need for the customer to accept a loan to the full value of this amount, they may if they wish elect to borrow a lesser amount. The pawn-broker issues along with the money a ticket which sets forth all the details of the transaction and at any time the customer may redeem the pledge by paying back the loan plus the standard interest. If the goods are not redeemed within a year and a day of the pledging then the pawn-broker becomes the legal owner of the goods and he may dispose of them in any way he thinks fit. At any time during the year the customer may sell the ticket to a third party who then may redeem the pledge under the same condition as the original owner.

On the November 18 Oscar Slater called at Liddell's pawnshop in Sauchiehall Street to pawn a gold, cresent shaped brooch studded with three rows of diamonds. Slater was already known to the manager, Peter McLaren, for he had pawned some other jewellery a few days earlier. On that occasion Slater had used the name Anderson but McLaren knew him by his more common name for he remembered him as being a customer from some years back. Slater had been using the pawnshop on and off since 1901.

McLaren valued the brooch at £100, well above the sum Slater was asking, £20. Slater then used part of the £20 to redeem some of the items he had pawned earlier. The entire transaction is suggestive of nothing more than Slater changing his stock. The fact that Slater was using a false name in no way interested the pawnbroker, most of his customers tended to use false names to hide their embarrassment.

In the days before the safety razor blade the barber did a lot more shaving than he does today. There was, however, a rather nasty skin disease prevalent at that time and it was believed, quite correctly, that the condition was transmitted from face to face via the brush, soap and shaving-pot. As a consequence of this men who used the barber regularly used to supply their own equipment which was kept at the shop. The barbers, naturally, welcomed this trend for it made for a captive customer. A common sight in those days in the barber's shop was line after line of shaving accessories hanging on the wall, each with a tag identifying the owner.

Shortly after moving into 69 St Georges Road Slater elected to have his daily shave at Bramber's, a barber's shop at Charing Cross. To the usual accessories Slater added a bottle of after-shave which made certain that, if the barber already did not know it, his new customer was quite definitely a foreign gentleman. No self-respecting Scotsman would ever use scent. One morning early in December after some discussion about the allegedly ragged state of his moustache Slater instructed the barber to shave it off. It was an act of vanity that was to cost Slater his freedom.

Hugh Cameron was a bookmaker's clerk and probably Slater's best friend in Glasgow. His association with Slater went back for some years and Cameron had been among the first with whom Slater had made contact with on his return at the beginning of November. Cameron knew that Slater was a pimp and that the woman he was living with was an active prostitute but this knowledge seems not to have bothered him. He also knew that Slater was passing himself off as Anderson but this too he accepted as being normal. It was through Cameron that Slater became a member of the Sloper Club although in truth it was not too difficult to obtain membership. These clubs, attracting as they did a fair number of petty criminals, were always borderline cases as far as the police were concerned. They opened and closed with monotonous regularity and the Sloper Club itself had only been opened for a few weeks. It too was closed a few weeks later.

Nearly every day for the few weeks that Slater was in Glasgow he and Cameron met but it can hardly be said that they were leading a riotous life. As Cameron himself described it, "We employed ourself by filling in the time, such as going to the skating rink in the afternoons, and then going on to a music hall in the evening, and from there to the Sloper Club." In fact a boring sort of life.

Early in December Slater received a couple of letters which were to strongly influence his future movements. The first letter was from his old partner in America, Devoto. His partner had moved to San Francisco which was then rebuilding after the earthquake and there were plenty of opportunities for a well run gambling club. Devoto urged Slater to join him. The second letter was from a fellow pimp in London called Freedman. The letter said that Slater's wife had been in London looking for him and that she had contacted Freedman whom she apparently knew. Slater feared that Freedman had told his wife that her husband was in Glasgow and in this he was probably right. A move then, out of Glasgow, seemed to be a good idea.

There was not a lot of money around in Glasgow due to the slump that year and whatever expectations Slater had harboured clearly they had not been realised. From early December then Slater set about preparing to go to America.

The first problem to be taken care of was that of the flat for which he had signed an eighteen month lease.

Had he have wished he could have simply walked away for the factor would hardly be likely to pursue him to the west coast of America. Similarly as his furniture was on hire-purchase he could just have returned it. For some reason Slater did not take either of these two courses. What he did was write to Freedman offering him the flat and contents as a going concern. Freedman replied accepting the offer, telling him that he would send two girls to take over.

Slater confirmed his intentions to his friend Cameron and gave him his future address in America. He could be contacted c/o Caesar's Cafe, 554 Broadway, San Francisco. At the time he also offered Cameron a commission if he could sell the gold and diamond brooch. Cameron accepted the commission but he had no better success than Slater. All this took place during the first two weeks of December.

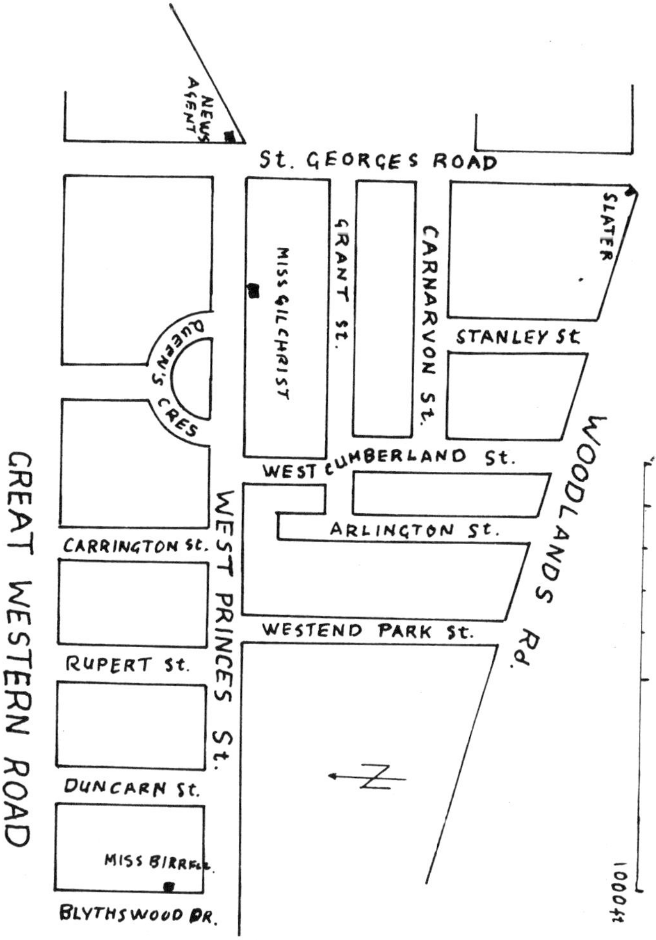

Map of general area (to scale)

CHAPTER 4

Monday, December 21, was just another day in the Gilchrist household. At about nine o'clock in the morning Helen wakened Miss Gilchrist and served her breakfast in bed. It was tea and toast and possibly a boiled egg. Of late Miss Gilchrist had been complaining of feeling tired in the mornings and she now seldom rose until noon. Lunch was served after mid-day and at about two o'clock the old lady went out. It was getting close to the end of the year and she had some bills to pay and she also wished to have a few words with the house factor about the fact that the flat was still empty. With winter now on and with the prospects of frost she had no wish to be flooded out with burst pipes. She returned to her flat at about four-thirty and looked into the kitchen. Helen was entertaining another maid to tea but her mistress raised no objections. She retired to her sitting-room to read until supper time.

The front door of the flat was fitted with three locks, not an uncommon arrangement in Glasgow flats even today. One lock was of the Yale type, that is to say it could be opened from the inside by a lever but it required a key if opened from the outside. The second lock was a Chubb dead-lock which required a key on both sides. The third lock was a common lock so called because it was fitted as standard to all doors. The common lock was actually a double lock, a dead lock operated by a key and a live lock operated by a simple knob. Thus if the door was merely pulled shut then it was held closed by the live part of the common lock and the yale lock which of course required a key to open from the outside.

At seven o'clock—almost precisely—Helen left the flat to buy an evening paper from a shop in St Georges Road, a round trip of approximately five minutes. Although she would only be gone for a few minutes she nevertheless took care to turn the key in the Chubb. At the entrance to the close she also took care to pull the close door shut as she left.

From the close to the corner of West Princes Street with St Georges Road is exactly seventy-five yards or just about a minute's walk and as she reached the corner Helen met a policeman in plain clothes. There had been a number of burglaries in the area during the previous fortnight and some of the uniformed police had been sent out on patrol in plain clothes in an attempt to capture the thieves. Helen knew the policeman and she stopped to talk to him in spite of the fact that it was now raining quite heavily. The couple spoke for nearly ten minutes until the passing of another policeman brought the conversation to a hurried conclusion.

Helen now continued on her way to the newsagent and when she got there she insisted that nothing less than the final edition of the Evening Citizen would do. The shopkeeper assured her that had she been a moment earlier she would have seen the final edition being delivered. With this assurance, Helen paid over the half-penny and received her copy.

In fact the paper was hardly worth the buying that evening. Most of it consisted of advertisements for Christmas and New Year. Santa at a large department store, rocking horses on sale for 5/- (25p), cases of whisky (a dozen bottles to the case) for £1.50 per case. The coming pantomimes in the various theatres were also heavily advertised.

There was no real big news stories that evening. A motor company, Humber, was in financial difficulties and was expected to go under. Horatio Bottemly was once more in the dock facing a conspiracy to fraud charge, and once more he would be found not guilty. Manoeuvres were being held in the south of England and an aeroplane was being used to spot the *enemy*. The plane was being flown by a young army captain who had not only paid for his own flying lessons but had provided the plane as well. In the event it turned out to be a costly experiment for the plane crashed and was a write-off. There was also a story from Austria reporting that a protestant minister had been eaten by a wolf. Whether this had any religious significance is not stated.

Local news was also very thin. Public relief was expected to reach an all time high that winter due to the slump. There was a moral crusade taking place in Paisley which does not seem to have had any lasting benefit. There was also a think piece which asked the question, is the Panto finished? The writer seemed to think that it was, which only goes to show how wrong you can be.

Back at the flat Miss Gilchrist was lying on her back with a rug covering her face. She no longer had any interest in the news.

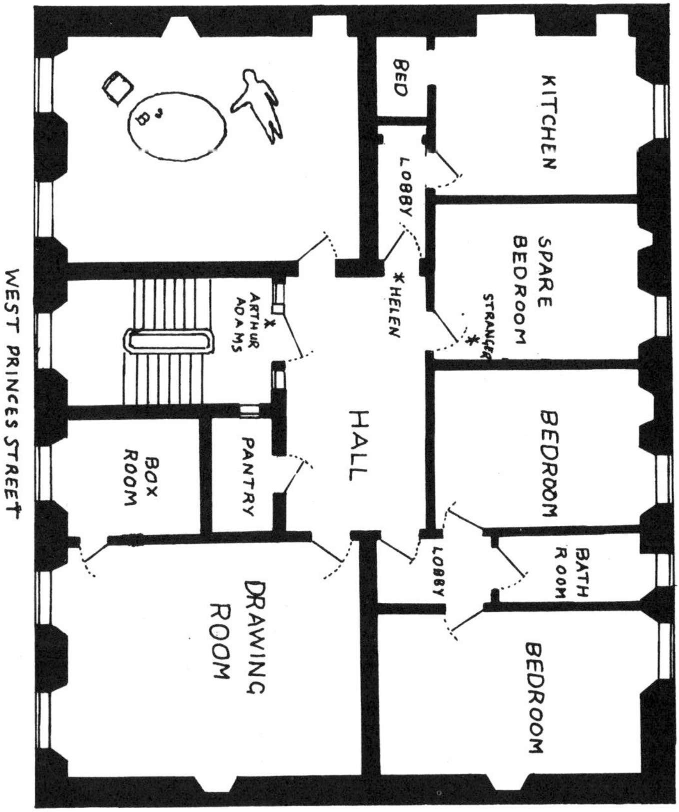

Layout of flat

CHAPTER 5

Arthur Adams lived with his mother and five sisters in the ground floor flat immediately below the flat occupied by Miss Gilchrist. In layout both flats were pretty much the same. By profession Arthur was a musician, he played the flute, and his eldest sister was also a musician, she taught music at the flat. Surrounded as he was by females Arthur comes across as being something of a wimp completely dominated by the women of the family.

There was one daughter in the family who was married, Rowena, and the fates had conspired that on that particular Monday night, at about five minutes to seven, Rowena should be paying a call on her family. As she approached her mother's front door she saw a man standing outside the door leading to the upstairs flats. Because of the recent burglaries Rowena gave the man what she described as a "hard look" but hard look or not the man did not seem to be unduely preturbed.

The reason why Rowena was paying a visit to her mother's house that evening had something to do with the making of a dress for one of her sisters. The festive season was at hand and it was a time for parties. Rowena had something of a reputation where the sartorial arts were concerned. As a result of all this if we included the dress-maker then the complement of women in the house that evening had risen to eight. Is it any wonder then that Arthur fled to the peace and quiet of the dining-room to read his paper and the dining-room was immediately below the room used by Miss Gilchrist as her sitting-room.

Shorty after seven o'clock, just a minute or two after, Arthur heard a noise as though someone or something had fallen to the floor of the room above. This noise was followed almost immediately by a number of sharp raps over a period of a minute or two. Had he been alone then it almost certain that Arthur would have ignored it but it so happened that just at that moment another of his sisters, Laura, entered the room and she too heard the noise. Some weeks earlier Laura had been talking to Miss Gilchrist and her elderly neighbour had confessed to feeling frightened when left alone in the house. It was probably all the talk about the recent spate of burglaries that brought the subject up. Whatever the reason Laura had told Miss Gilchrist that if she was ever alone and needed assistance then she should try and rap on the floor and help would come from downstairs.

At forty years of age Arthur was no hero and so when his sister instructed him to go up stairs to find out whether help was needed he did so with the greatest of reluctance. He feared the worst and was all too well aware that he was ill-equiped to meet any possible challenges. Nevertheless, armed with a key to the close door—they had a key to give them access to the back court—Arthur set off to do his sister's bidding.

The first surprise came when he found the close door to be lying open, it was always closed. Resolutely Arthur pressed on up the stairs to the first floor landing. The door to Miss Gilchrist's flat was flanked on either side by two broad strips of coloured glass and through the glass darkly he could see that the gas light in the hall was burning. Arthur applied his ear to the door, the interior was quiet. He rang the bell two or three times but to no avail. There was still no sound or sign of any movement in the hall. As befits a coward Arthur took this to mean that everything was alright and so he returned downstairs.

Back in his house Arthur was faced by all of his sisters reinforced by the presence of the dress-maker. To their cries of disgust he was immediately forced to return to the flat above and this time he was to stay until he had spoken to either Miss Gilchrist or the maid. Poor Arthur was learning a bitter lesson that night. There was more to life than just getting your shirts washed and ironed.

Helen had made her way back to the flat through the rain and she too was surprised to find the door to the close lying open. She also noted wet footprints on the first few treads of the stair. As she hurried up the stair she could hear the sound of a bell being rung furiously.

Arthuir told her as she arrived on the landing of his fears for her mistress and of the noises he had heard but Helen treated his fears lightly. As she unlocked the door she explained to Arthur that they had been having trouble with the pulley—a rack suspended from the ceiling for the drying and airing of laundry and raised and lowered by a system of ropes—and that the noise that he had heard had probably been that of the pulley falling. Helen was remarkably calm and the only thing which might have indicated any fears that she may have had was that she was speaking in rather a loud voice.

As the door swung open Helen stepped into the hall and inclined slightly to the left (see plan of house) and crossed the hall in the direction of the short lobby which led to the kitchen. The maid had just about reached the entrance to this short lobby when the door to the spare bedroom, immediately opposite the front door, swung open and a man stepped out into the hall. For an instance the man was framed in the doorway by the light in the bedroom and then briskly, but not excitedly, he crossed the hall, squeezed by Arthur standing in the front door—Arthur actually had to move slightly to permit him to pass—ran down the stairs and disappeared into the night. Helen, apparently, alerted by the sound of the bedroom door being opened glanced over he shoulder until the man disappeared and then continued on into the kitchen.

In the kitchen Helen turned up the gas light which she had left on a peep before leaving the flat. Everything was in order and she said so when she reappeared once more in the hall. She now turned her attention to the spare bedroom and when she re-emerged it was again to tell Arthur that everything seemed to be alright. She does not seem to have noticed that a small wooden box which sat on a dressing-table had been forced open and that the papers it contained had been scattered around. Finally Helen entered the sitting-room only to emerge a moment later, white-faced, to tell the waiting Arthur that something dreadful had happened to her mistress.

Bracing himself for the shock Arthur entered the sitting-room followed by Helen. On the floor next to the table, the head pointing towards the fireplace and the feet towards the door, lay the body of Miss Gilchrist, her head mercifully covered by a rug. Hesitantly, Arthur advanced towards the body, all around were the physical signs of violence, blood and bits of tissue. Sickened, Arthur took Helen by the arm and led her out of the room.

The couple now hurried down the stairs into the street and after telling Helen to remain there until he returned Arthur set off in the direction of St Georges Road in the forlorn hope of catching up with the stranger he had seen in the hall.

CHAPTER 6

Constable Francis Brien was a policeman whose beat covered that part of West Princes Street that included Miss Gilchrist's flat. His duty that night had started at six o'clock and would last through until two in the morning. Although he had only been on duty for little more than an hour he had already passed along West Princes Street twice and was in the process of his third pass when he met the excited Arthur Adams. Together the two men hurried along the street but when they arrived at the close Helen was nowhere to be seen. Leaving the policeman to guard the entry Arthur dashed across the road to the home of a Dr Adams, no relative, just in case it was still possible to do something for his elderly neighbour.

Dr Adams, as befits a medical man, did not panic when Arthur burst into his surgery. The first thing that he did was to telephone the police and only then did he collect his bag and accompany Arthur back across the road. In the sitting-room the doctor rapidly took stock of the situation. The old woman, whom he knew by sight but not professionally, was too far gone for any help that he could offer. This had been apparent from the moment he had lifted the corner of the rug covering the head and had seen the hole in the skull. No one could have possibly survived such damage. Having satisfied himself on that score Adams took the opportunity to look around the room and what he saw would be earnestly discussed long after he was dead.

Organisationally the police force in Glasgow was divided into a number of separate divisions, each division under the direction of a Chief Superintendent, responsible for the policing of its area. Theoretically, the Central Division was no different from the other divisions but in practice it had become in time the premier division in the city. This had been unavoidable given that most of the major crime took place in the city centre and that the division shared quarters with the

Headquarter staff. Thus although the murder of Miss Gilchrist fell within the area controlled by the Western Division the detectives of the Central CID were involved in the case right from the beginning.

West Princes Street fell, just, within the area of the Western Division and it was on their shoulders that the task of conducting the initial investigation fell. The first senior officer to arrive at the scene of the crime was Inspector Pyper, he had made good time for the telephone call was logged at 7.25pm and he was at the flat just after 7.45pm. Pyper was 51 years of age with thirty years service in the force, half of that as a detective. From the only photograph known of him he was a man who sported an immense black beard so that he looked like an old fashioned preacher.

When Pyper had joined the force in 1878 it had been little more than a watch service designed to protect the wealthier citizens during the hours of darkness against the predations of those without respect for private property. For this work a strong arm and thick skull was all that was required and any detection was left to the office of the Procurator-fiscal to attend to. In his time Pyper had seen a great deal of change more especially in the emergence of the Criminal Investigation Department. Pyper was by no means the brightest of policemen but he had a great deal of experience.

As Pyper entered the room he automatically noted the details of the scene. It was a large room some 20ft. by 18ft. With most of the wall to his left consisting entirely of window. The room was well furnished but not over so. Against the wall, to his right, stood a handsome sideboard and on either side of the fire-place were two small easy chairs with some other chairs against the walls around the room. In the centre of the room, directly under the gas chandelier, stood an oval dining table with four chairs arranged around it. All the walls were covered with paintings in their heavy gilt frames. The body of the dead woman had not been disturbed and it was lying with its head pointing towards the fire-place and about eighteen inches from the fender. The feet were pointing towards the door and the body was lying some two feet from the edge of the table.

With Dr Adams hovering in the background, Pyper dropped to one knee in order to examine the wound more closely. It was not a pleasant sight. Straightening up he asked the doctor a couple of questions about the probable speed of death and then, much to the doctor's chagrin, dismissed him from the room.

On the easy chair next to the body Constable Brien drew the attention of the Inspector to a red coloured skin rug which the constable said had been covering the head of the victim and which had been removed by the doctor. Part of the rug was heavily soaked in blood on its hairy side and there was traces of blood on the reverse side. Near to the body on the floor lay the upper plate of a set of false teeth made from gold and near to that there lay a half sovereign. Pyper told the constable to place the teeth and the coin on the mantlepiece where they would be safe.

The table yielded little of interest. Along side an open magazine lay a pair of gold frame spectacles giving the appearance of the owner having been interrupted while reading. Pyper cast around for any sign of a possible weapon, he examined the fire-irons and the ornaments on the mantlepiece but none of these likely objects had been used for the purpose. With the room yielding no obvious clues Pyper turned to the two witnesses.

When Arthur Adams had vanished along West Princes Street in hot pursuit he had left Helen standing at the door to the close. Seeing her alone some of the Adams sisters had ventured out to suggest that she should wait with them inside their house until the police arrived. But Helen could not be persuaded and instead she set off in the direction of Rupert Street which was just a few yards along the road. Margaret Birrell lived with her lodger in Rupert Street and it was to the niece to tell her of her aunt's death that Helen went. With mounting horror Miss Birrell listened to what Helen had to tell her and as she told her story they were joined by the lodger, Charles Cowan, still in his braces and with traces of lather on his face from the bathroom where he had been shaving. Margaret told Helen that she should return to the flat and that she and Cowan would join her there as soon as possible. One would have thought that Margaret, at least, would have gone immediately to the scene of the crime?

Pyper first turned his attention towards Helen whom he found to be a remarkably cool and calm witness. The fact that the Inspector saw fit later to make this observation would suggest by inference that Arthur was not cool and calm. His first task above all was to get a good description of the mysterious man who had been in the flat. Here Helen was of little help for, as she said, she had only caught the briefest glimpse of the man as he had crossed the hall and most of that had been of his back. Because the man had moved with such self-assurance she had assumed that he was there by the permission of her mistress and no maid could ever ask a guest what he was about.

Arthur Adams was a bit more helpful. The stranger was about 5ft-9 inches tall, aged 30-40, and reasonably well-built. He had been wearing dark trousers and light overcoat, possible fawn or grey in colour. He may or may not have been wearing a hat and he was either clean shaven or if he had a moustache then it was not immediately obvious. Generally speaking the man looked respectable, possibly a commercial traveller or clerk. It was a description that would have fitted a large number of men. Still it was all that Pyper had to go on for the moment and this was the discription circulated to all the police in Glasgow in the immediate aftermath of the murder.

As the time passed Inspector Pyper was joined by other senior officers, right from the beginning it was being treated as an important case. The first to arrive was Superintendent Douglas of the Western Division CID and Pyper's immediate superior. He was quickly followed by Chief Superintendent Orr, the officer in charge of the Western Division. Finally they were joined by Superintendent Ord, the officer in charge of

Central Division CID. Ord had been hard to locate for he was off duty and attending a meeting of the Old Glasgow Society. This historical society is still in existence and meets regularly during the winter months. Ord had acted quickly the moment that he had been informed of the murder and his first order was that no detective in his division should book-off without his permission. His next order was to recall those detectives who had already booked-off and that every available detective should be out on the streets to see what they could find.

The four officers, Pyper, Douglas, Orr and Ord now met in the kitchen of the flat to discuss all that was known about the murder at that point. A close examination of the flat had shown that all the windows, with the exception of the kitchen window, were closed and locked. The kitchen window had been opened a couple of inches at the top but there was no sign of that window having been used to effect an entry. Similarly all the locks on the door to the flat were working and none bore any signs of having been forced. The conclusion then was clear enough, the murderer had been admitted into the flat.

But Miss Gilchrist would have hardly been likely to have admitted a stranger into the flat while she was alone so the second conclusion suggested itself. The murderer had been a person known to Miss Gilchrist. The initial scenario then, seemed to be that the murderer had concealed himself, probably in one of the closes on the opposite side of the street, and watched for Helen to leave the house. He had then crossed the road, rang the bell and been admitted. This also suggested that the murderer was acquainted with the movements of the household. So the person they were looking for was a male friend or relative of the dead woman.

It was when they turned to consider the motive, however, that the case started to become more complicated. Helen had told Pyper that her mistress had a considerable collection of jewellery hidden mainly in the pockets of dresses and coats hanging in the wardrobe in the spare bedroom. With Helen, Pyper had searched the wardrobe and found a fortune in jewels. Although she could not be certain it seemed that only one item was missing, a gold, cresent shaped brooch with a single row of diamonds which had been lying in a small dish on the dressing-table. But in the same dish there had also been three rings and in another dish a gold watch, none of which had been touched. Similarly the false teeth and the spectacles were also of some value and yet these too had been left. Had robbery been the motive then the thief had shown a surprising lack of commitment to his purpose. While the interruption by Arthur Adams might well explain why no attempt had been made to search the wardrobe, it could not explain why the other items, lying as it were at hand, were left untouched.

Interestingly, later the police would endeavour to play down the value of these items by claiming first that there was only one ring and then that they were relatively worthless. Because these items were never particularly identifed we have no way of knowing which ring is which in the list prepared later by the valuator. We do know, however, that the cheapest ring in the collection was valued at £10 which means that the thief turned his back on a considerable sum.

Another possibility that had to be considered was that the murderer was not after the jewels at all. A small box kept in the spare bedroom and used to hold documents of various descriptions had been opened and its contents scattered. Could it have been, then, that what the murderer had been really after was some paper, perhaps of an incriminating nature? Was Miss Gilchrist some kind of blackmailer who had arranged that her victim should call while the maid was out of the house? While the theory was attractive the facts seemed to be against it. The only papers apparently kept in the box were household bills and other such similar papers, there was absolutely no sign of any papers of a personal nature. Nevertheless, at this stage such a possibility was not being ruled out.

The subsequent history of this box is quite interesting. Although it was an exhibit and constantly mentioned at the trial very little was actually revealed about it. For instance whether the box had a lock fitted to it was never made quite clear although perhaps this was plain enough to the court. And if it had a lock which had been locked then had the box been forced open? This again was never made clear. Thus the claim made by certain newspapers that the box had been forced has never really been proved.

There was one other option to be considered. Although still lacking any pathology report—Professor Glaister, the pathologist, had been informed but he was entertaining friends to dinner that night and so had refused to come—the wounds to the head had been so vicious as to suggest that the murderer had been determined beyond reason that his victim should die. The botched up robbery then could merely have been an attempt to confuse the police. Curiously enough the officer most in favour of this last scenario was Inspector Pyper. To his credit he alone seems to have realised that there was something not quite right about the murder of Miss Gilchrist although for the life of him he could not put his doubts into words.

As the news of the murder spread the street outside the flat became crowded with people. Most were just idle bystanders but the press was well represented and more than willing to interview anyone who had anything to say either about the murder or the victim. It has to be said to their credit that on the whole they managed to get the essential facts of the case right. The next morning the Daily Record carried what was possible the best account of the murder.

According to the Record Helen was a "handsome young woman" who, when she had discovered the body of her dead mistress, had shouted out to Arthur Adams, "my mistress is murdered—catch that man." Not perhaps wholly correct but near enough. The Record then goes on to describe in great detail the scene in the house which suggests that the reporter had somehow managed to get inside. The reporter claims that the box containing the papers had been forced and that a box of matches of a brand not widely sold in Glasgow had also been found. He also identifies the murder weapon as being an axe. While this last point was completely wrong the nature of the wounds were such as to have made an axe a likely weapon so that his mistake is understandable.

Having reported the fact the Record then goes on to speculate as to the possible motives for the murder. Having noted the strong possibility that the murderer had been known to his victim the story goes on to comment about the jewellery which had not been taken and links it to the mysterious death of a dog belonging to the victim which had died some weeks earlier. This last piece of information could only have come from Helen and it could only have been volunteered at that. As far as the Record was concerned they had no doubt but that the murder had been premeditated which puts them in line with Pyper's thinking.

The story finishes with a report of the arrest of two men by detectives from the Central CID and that an identification parade was being arranged for later in the day. These two men were later released.

The next morning all the newspaper carried a first description of the alleged murderer. Age 25-30. Dark haired, clean shaven, fawn overcoat, cloth cap. No height or build given.

CHAPTER 7

Between the two world wars Sir Bernard Spilsbury, the pathologist, dominated every notable murder trial in England, many of which it has to be said owed their noteriety to his presence. The announcement that Spilsbury was to appear for either the prosecution or the defence—it made no difference for he was free-lance and his services were available to whoever could get to him first—was a guarantee that the public benches would be filled. In this respect he was a bit like a film star. The press loved him because, having a fine sense for the dramatic, he always provided good copy. In common with many others in the medical profession at that time he had more than his fair share of arrogance and his reputation for crushing opposing counsel was legendary. Many an eminent counsel gave up hope when he learned that Spilsbury was to be called for the opposite side.

Nowadays, with the advances in medical science, pathology has become much more a matter of fact rather than of opinion and a jaundice eye is now cast backwards at some of Sir Bernard's most successful cases. He has been weighed in the balance of history and found to be wanting. There would seem to be little doubt but that in some of his cases where his opinion was crucial the wrong decision was arrived at and that the innocent paid the penalty for his arrogance and the public willingness to believe the unsupported word of the expert.

Spilsbury, of course, was not unique, neither was he the first. One of the earlier pathologists who possible served as a role model for Spilsbury was the pathologist to whom the Glasgow police turned in time of murder, John Glaister, Professor of Forensic Medicine at the University of Glasgow. When he had been informed of the murder of Miss Gilchrist the night previous he had imperiously told the police that he would attend to the matter the next morning. The police dutifully waited.

Professor Glaister and his colleague, Dr Galt, arrived at the flat at 10am the following morning when the body had already been dead for at least fifteen hours. After noting details of the room his report gets down to the facts:—

". . . On the carpet rug in front of the fire-place the body was lying. The head was pointing diagonally to the fire-place, and the feet towards the dining-room door. The right arm was extended at right angles to the body, the left leg was crossed over the right leg.

"Without disturbing the body, it was observed that the head and face had been very much smashed. There were wounds on the right cheek extending to the mouth, wounds on the right forehead, and on the right side of the head. There was a deep hole on the left side of the face between the eye socket and the left ear.

"The left eyeball was entirely missing, having either been driven into the cavity of the brain or having been gouged out. The right eye was partially torn out of its socket by the deep fractures on the right side of the brow. There was much blood on and among the hair of the head. On the carpet beneath the head on both sides was a considerable amount of clotted blood, and the fluid blood had soaked into the substance of the rug. Between the head and the fender of the fire-place a piece of brain tissue weighing about three-quarters of an ounce, as well as smaller pieces, and several pieces of bone covered with blood was found.

"The fire-irons were in their place. They were bespattered with blood as was also the grate and the fire-bars. The legs of some of the chairs in the neighbourhood of the coal scuttle were also bespattered with blood. All the signs indicated that the injuries had been inflicted in the neighbourhood of where the body was found lying, and that the injuries had been produced by the very forcible application of some instrument."

Of course the examination in the house was not a full examination, that would come later at the Royal Infirmary. Its purpose was to allow the pathologist to view the body in position in the hope that something could be gleaned that might be useful. Glaister's message to Pyper was not very encouraging. According to the pathologist it appeared that Miss Gilchrist had been standing facing her assailent when he had struck the first blow. This blow had been to the left eye and was undoubtedly the blow that killed her. Having delivered the first blow and with his victim lying on the floor the murderer had apparently crossed over to the side-board, picked up the red skin rug and thrown it over the head of Miss Gilchrist. He had then delivered a regular frenzy of blows to the right hand side of the head, somewhere between 30-60 blows. What Glaister was saying, although all the indications is that even he did not appreciate its importance, is that the attack on Miss Gilchrist had been divided into two distinct and separate phases. The initial attack which killed her, the placing of the rug over the head, and the final series of blows.

The first examination by Glaister and his colleague, even by the standards of 1908, left a great deal to be desired. As the professor himself said, "it is quite obvious that there must have been spurting of blood when the wounds were caused over the temporal arteries." Now the wound to the left eye which had been so vicious as to smash the bone of the socket making an entry to brain cavity was the equivalent of severing a temporal artery and that blow had apparently been delivered while Miss Gilchrist had been standing. One would have expected then that the spurt of blood would have delivered a scattering over quite a large area of the room and quite possible marking the surface of the table. In fact the only signs of blood and tissue were all contained within a very small area of an arc between the head and the fire-place and nothing was found further than about two feet from the head.

What Glaister was saying then, in effect, was that by some remarkable coincidence although the first blows were delivered some five to six feet from the second set of blows—Miss Gilchrist being standing and then having staggered backwards before falling to the floor—all the visible signs of the attack were confined to one small area. That does not make any sense.

Glaister's account becomes even less tenable when one considers the remarkable lack of blood around the body. Although he does not quantify the amount the only blood he notes is some blood around the head which had soaked through to the underside of the carpet. At the most this could not have mounted to much more than half a pint and yet in view of the injuries two or three pints would have been reasonably expected.

Later that morning at the Royal Infirmary, Glaister carried his autopsy and his report was sent to the Procurator-fiscal. Briefly, apart from outlining the grim details of the injuries, it solved the mystery of the missing eyeball. The left eyeball had been driven through the socket into the brain cavity. The autopsy also revealed that the sternum or breast bone and three of the ribs had been fractured from which it was concluded that at one stage during the attack the murderer had knelt on the victim. There was also a confusing feature for there was a lack of consistency in the shape left by the weapon on the wounds. These impressions were so varied as to suggest that the weapon itself had been of an irregular shape and that the murderer had constantly changed his grip on the weapon. It was as though he had rotated it constantly in his hand.

For a woman of her advanced years Miss Gilchrist had been in excellent health. All her internal organs were healthy and functioning normally. In Glaister's opinion she could have looked forward to a few more years of life.

While at the flat Glaister had been given a auger—a metal tool for boring holes in wood somewhat similar to a corkscrew in shape although much larger—which had been found in the back-green when it had become light enough to search. The auger was seemingly stained with blood and with fibres sticking to it which were suggestive of grey hairs. Glaister subjected the auger to tests which showed that the alleged blood stains were in fact rust stains. The fibres were not identified. Nevertheless for the next few days this auger was retained as the murder weapon.

In fact there was a perfectly good explanation for the presence of the auger in the back-green. Behind the flat was an old engineering workshop which had been abandoned without being emptied of its contents and among these contents were a number of similar augers. As small boys will do they had forced an entry into the old workshop and one of their ploys was to throw the rubbish over the wall into the back-green. There is good reason for believing that Inspector Pyper at least knew of this but the knowledge did not affect the status of the auger as the weapon.

Thus by the end of the first day of the investigation the police had managed, or so they thought, to reconstruct at least in part the circumstances surrounding the death of Miss Gilchrist. The old woman had admitted the murderer into the house and had taken him into the sitting-room where she had stopped at the edge of the table and turned round to face her caller. The murderer had immediately struck her a blow which had knocked her down to the floor and killed her. The sound of her body falling had been the first noise to alarm her neighbours.

Of course the autopsy was not the only activity carried out that day as part of the investigation into the murder. Whenever a person, even of modest means, meets with a violent death the first question the police ask is, who profits? The police then in the person of Superintendent Douglas called on Miss Gilchrist's solicitor on the morning after the murder. The purpose of the visit was to examine any will the old lady might have made in order to find out who would inherit.

The question of the will and what it did or did not contain was to become the subject of much discussion in the press over the following days. Indeed one enterprising reporter from the Daily Record also called on the solicitor requesting a look at the will and was upset for some reason when shown the door. The fact that none of the reporters had seen the will was to be no bar to their speculations.

All the press over the next few days carried the story that Miss Gilchrist had made an alteration to her will shortly before she was murdered. This was apparently true although how they had managed to find out must be something of a mystery. I suspect that it had been pieced together from a number of different sources. But an altered will does not necessarily mean that someone has been struck out, it can just as well mean that someone has been added to the list. The speculation, however, which was freely floated by the press, was that for some reason a male relative had been cut out and that in a fit of rage he had killed the old woman. But do disappointed beneficiaries tend to bump off their rich relatives? Now it is not unknown for those who stand to benefit to take steps to speed up the normal process of nature but for those who know that they are to be disappointed such a course of action could only be self-defeating. A more likely reaction would be to endeavour with what time there may be left to worm one's way back into the good graces. The press were fishing in a very shallow pool but it is quite amazing just how long that particular story has lasted.

Wills, of course, once probated are public property and therefore who inherited what could not remain a secret for long. Miss Gilchrist's friend, Mr Robertson, was appointed executor and for his duties he was to receive a handsome carved oak chair. His wife was also granted the choice of two diamond bracelets from the collection. Mrs Margaret Ferguson, a former maid, was left the contents of the wardrobe and her daughter, Marion, the God-child of Miss Gilchrist, the piano, the best bedroom suite in figured walnut, the bed linen and a painting of her God-mother. A Mr Stewart was to receive an oil painting by Hunt. All the remaining furniture and personal effects were to be sold.

Having disposed of her goods and chattels the will

now disposed of Miss Gilchrist's wealth. The interest from £2,000 suitably invested, was to be paid to Mrs Jane Birrell and on her death the capital was to be distributed among various charities. Margaret Birrell, not seemingly the same Margaret Birrell whom we have already met, was to receive £1,000 as were Margaret and Marion Ferguson. A Mr Johnston, Catherine Hunter and Eliza Lee were each to receive £500. An Anthony McCall was to receive £100 and finally, if she was still in her employment at the time of her death, Helen Lambie was to receive £20 or the equivalent of 18 months salary.

After all bequests had been met the residue was to go to Marion Ferguson. A codicile was later added to this will, which had been written in May, 1908, on November 20 of the same year. Marion Ferguson was no longer to be the sole legatee of the residue. It was now to be divided equally with her sister.

Quite clearly, in spite of the codicile, Marion Ferguson, the God-daughter, was the main beneficiary of the will followed by her mother. At a rough calculation Marion received something like £3,000, or possibly more, in cash. Not a bad nest-egg for a girl whose father was a guard on the railway. Only three members of Miss Gilchrist's direct family were remembered. It would seem then that the press were only partly right in their speculation about some members of the immediate family having been disinherited shortly before the murder. The disinheriting had taken place months earlier in May.

The rumours regarding the relationship between Miss Gilchrist and her former maid, Margaret Ferguson, were, perhaps not unnaturally, fueled by the contents of the will. Especially the gifting of the bed and the bed-linen to Marion Ferguson. It was being claimed as being the indisputable truth that Margeret was the illegitimate daughter of Miss Gilchrist. The real truth was, I believe, that Miss Gilchrist merely wanted to leave her money to a person who would appreciate it most. She made a poor girl a comparatively rich girl.

It is at this point that a new actor enters our drama, an actor who would later become one of the stars although at first it looked as though all that fate had alloted him was a bit-part.

Detective John Trench was one of Glasgow's young and upcoming detectives and indeed it is probably no exageration to claim that he would become the best known policeman in Scotland. Trench came to prominence in what was to become known as the Broughty Ferry Murder. Broughty Ferry was, and still is, a small town or village outside Dundee and generally populated with the better off business men of the city.

In November, 1912, Miss Milne, a resident of Broughty Ferry, was found murdered in her home and subsequently a tramp called Warner was detained in Maidstone, England, on suspicion of having committed the murder. Initially the local police were not making any headway and Trench, who was seemingly promoted to lieutenant at that time, was sent to give them whatever assistance he could. On Warner's arrest he was photographed and on the basis of this photograph he was identified as being the man seen near the scene of the crime by five witnesses. Trench was sent to Maidstone to bring back Warner and while there he had the opportunity to hear Warner's side of the story. Warner claimed that he had in fact been in Belgium at the time of the killing and as proof he said that he had pawned a waistcoat there. Trench crossed the channel, found the pawnshop and proved Warner's alibi.

But all this was still four years in the future and in 1908 Trench was still just a detective-constable although he was seemingly already marked down as a detective with a future. A few hours after the murder of Miss Gilchrist, Trench had been at the flat but had not got any further than the first floor landing. There was nothing significant in this for the number of people being allowed into the actual scene of the murder was being heavily restricted and Trench was a very junior ranking detective. The next day however, that is on the

Tuesday, Trench was sent by his superior, Superintendent Ord, to interview Margaret Birrell at her home. Obviously as Miss Birrell was a potentially important witness Trench must have thought that his commission was a bit strange, especially as he was not even a member of the Division in charge of the investigation. The significance of this interview will be dealt with later.

Another strange interview also took place that day. Douglas, Pyper and another detective went by taxi to interview a man but who and where was not disclosed at the time. All that can be assumed is that given the mode of transport used then the person interviewed obviously stayed at some distance from regular public transport. This too will be dealt with more fully at a later date.

By the time that the evening papers hit the streets there was already the first signs of a growing disquiet among the press. The reporters were becoming cynical about both the lack of any leads and the infantile description of the stranger in the hall. The only thing that was new was an unattributed police report claiming that, "the murderer had an interest in the affairs of Miss Gilchrist and that he had been determined to silence her forever." As the police at this stage still had not made up their minds as to the motive for the murder then it can only be assumed that they had floated the story in an attempt to lower the temperature.

CHAPTER 8

If Tuesday had been a bad day for the police, then Wednesday did not at first look as if it was going to be much better. The two men who had been arrested shortly after the murder were released and their place taken by a third suspect. This man, who was apparently never named, had been selling men's coats around the pubs and clubs, coats which at first were thought to have been stolen. A hurried identification parade quickly freed him.

One matter greatly exercising the minds of the police at that moment was the precise escape route taken by the stranger in the hall after he had left the flat. There were three such routes. Firstly, on leaving the close the man could have turned right along West Princes Street to St Georges Road, the trail unsuccessfully followed by Arthur Adams. Once in St Georges Road he would have the choice of a number of different tram cars to carry him clear of the scene. Secondly, the man could have turned left, walked along to West Cumberland Street and the on to Woodlands Road. Here too he would have a choice of a number of tram routes. Thirdly, from the close he could have left inclined across the street into Queens Crescent and on to the Great Western Road and once more to a number of tram routes.

On all these three roads tram cars bound for different destinations were passing along at the rate of one and two a minute, they were all main transport routes to and from the centre of the city. Dozens of tram conductors whose trams had passed between 7.15 and 7.45 were interviewed but to no avail. No conductor could remember any suspicious passenger that evening.

Constable McGimpsey, a detective attached to the Northern Division, lived near to the scene of the crime in Seamore Street. Late on the Wednesday afternoon he had been leaving his house to go on duty when he met a neighbour, Barbara Barrowman. Mrs Barrowman was highly embarrassed at having to approach a policeman, especially as what she had to tell she already thought was rubbish. She had a daughter, Mary, fourteen years of age, who worked as a message girl for a bootmaker and who had come home late on the Monday night.

"I remember on Monday, December 21, Mary coming home late that night. She said that an old lady had been murdered in West Princes Street, and she had went down from the Band of Hope with some of the children to see where it was, as she had seen a gentleman coming out of the close, and she wondered what he had been doing. She said that she did not know that a murder had happened then, but she said that it was out of the same close that the man came. She said she was sure that she would know his face if she saw him again."

Had McGimpsey brushed his neighbour off then it would have been understandable after getting such a garbled statement. But he did not ignore it and when he reported for duty he passed the message along to his superiors. Later that evening two detectives were sent to interview Mary Barrowman.

Mary was the adopted daughter of Mr and Mrs Barrowman, her mother having died at the birth. Mr Barrowman was employed as a labourer in an iron foundry, a low paid occupation, and Mary had received a minimal education. In 1908 she was fourteen years of age and with not much of a future to look forward to. But Mary also, I suspect, aspired to leadership. In the Band of Hope among the younger girls Mary was the boss. It is also clear from her subsequent behaviour that Mary also enjoyed the limelight and liked to be noticed.

The story Mary told the detectives was that on the Monday night, the night of the murder, she had been sent by her employer, Colin Maccallum, to deliver a pair of boots to a Mr Howat, of Cleveland Street. Mary worked from 9am until 8pm and on that night it had been seven o'clock or there abouts when she had started on her delivery. At around 7.15 or slightly later she was walking along West Princes Street:—

"When I came opposite the close a man came running out of it and knocked up against me. He wore a fawn overcoat, a dark suit of clothes and a Donegal hat. He was wearing dark brown boots. He ran towards West Cumberland Street, and I could see he turned down there. I was just at the lamp-post near the close when this happened. I saw him coming out of the close. I saw him coming down the steps. He was coming very fast. When he came down to the foot of the steps he turned towards me. I did not see anything in his hands."

For a tired young girl, in a quiet street, in the dark, walking in the rain, carrying a parcel, her mind fixed on the promised joys of the Band of Hope, Mary had seen and remembered an amazing amount of detail. But how much help was this evidence at this time? Actually not very much for it contradicted evidence that the police already had. Mary went on to describe how after she had seen this man she had stood and watched him turn into West Cumberland Street which is about the same distance from the close in the opposite direction as is St Georges Road where presumably Mary was heading for. As Arthur Adams was claiming that he followed the stranger down the stairs within a minute then why had he not seen Mary who by her own words must have been still standing at or near to the close? One witness was clearly contradicting the other.

The real reason why the police first gave credence to Mary's story was that it took the press temporarily off their backs. All the evening papers that night were carrying articles severely critical of the lack of progress being made in bringing someone to book for the murder. The criticism undoubtedly would have continued in the following day's papers—one paper had already criticised the police for "occupying the position of those who are content to wait for something to happen", and without Mary the police had nothing new to offer.

In the background there was also a further threat

looming. Pressure was being brought upon the Chief Constable to take the case out of the hands of the Western Division and to put it into the hands of the Central Division CID.

The funeral of Miss Gilchrist took place on the Thursday afternoon from the private chapel of Wylie Lochhead, undertakers to the rich. The police put the story around that the funeral would leave her home and poor Arthur Adams, who was representing his family, had to sneak out of the back and climb walls in order to avoid leading the crowd to where the body was lying. As you would expect the funeral was attended by many of Glasgow's more prominent citizens and the Chief Constable was very much in attendance. At the hour of the funeral the streets between the chapel and the Eastern Necropolis over which the cortege would travel were cleared of traffic which brought disruption to the city centre. Miss Gilchrist was laid to rest in the Eta section of the graveyard, overlooking—as the press tactfully put it—the Ladywell. Delicacy forbade them to mention that the grave also overlooked Duke Street prison where the murderer, if he was ever caught, would be hanged for the crime.

It seems as though the prominent citizens present took the opportunity to have a word with the Chief Constable. When he returned to his office he issued his instructions which transferred the case from the Western to the Central Division. Superintendent Ord's neck was now firmly on the chopping-block.

Grave of Marion Gilchrist. Eta section, Eastern Necropolis.

CHAPTER 9

The Monday which saw the death of Miss Gilchrist had been a busy one for Oscar Slater. On that afternoon he posted a letter to the Post Office Savings Bank in London:—

Glasgow, 21st Dec. 1908—69 St Georges Road—Dear Sir, Enclosed you will find my savings book. Be kind enough to send me the money *at once* as I have an urgent call to America because my wife is ill. *If possible wire the money on* and I will pay all expenses here. Yours truely Adolph Anderson.

Oscar Slater was closing his bank account.

Slater had a pocket-watch which had recently been repaired by J. Dent of London. As a result of some accident the watch had started to lose time and so Slater had returned it to Dent's for further work. At 6.15pm on the evening of the 21st a telegram was handed into the telegraph office in Central Station:— Dent—Watchmaker—Trafalgar Square—London—If possible please send watch at once.—Oscar Slater.

The telegraph office in the Central Station was a busy office and even though the girl who had handled the message was later located she could not recall the transaction. The telegram could have been handed in by anyone. But Slater's next move would seem to confirm that it was he who had handed in the message.

From the Central Station to Johnston's billiard hall in Sauchiehall Street is approximately ten or so minutes walk and it was to the billiard hall that Slater went to meet a fellow German, Max Rattman. Rattman had been with Slater earlier that afternoon when he had gone to the pawnshop to raise a further £30 on the brooch he had pawned. His fellow German was acting on behalf of another who had expressed an interest in the brooch and Rattman was, as it were, examining the goods in advance. The agreement was, when the two men parted, that they should meet later in the day at the billiard hall with the prospective buyer. Slater arrived at about 6.30pm to find that the deal had fallen through and after a few minutes he left.

From the billiard hall to Slater's flat in St Georges Road is about fifteen minutes walk and to Miss Gilchrist's flat about a further five minutes. Thus when Slater left the billiard hall he had sufficient time to be at Miss Gilchrist's flat by seven o'clock but of course he claims he did nothing of the kind. He claims that he arrived at his flat shortly before seven and just in time for the evening meal.

On the Tuesday afternoon, that is the day after the death of Miss Gilchrist, Hugh Cameron was out shopping in the city centre with his wife. A fact, I fear, so rare that in itself it is worthy of being recorded in history. Near Central Station Cameron saw his friend Slater on the opposite side of the road and leaving his wife to make her own way home he crossed the road to join him. Slater was on his way to the offices of the Cunard Shipping Company to enquire about a passage to America. At the office he was offered the choice between the Lusitania sailing on the 26th from Liverpool or on the Campangia sailing on January 1. Undecided which ship to take Slater said that he would call back later.

While there Slater took advantage of Cunard's foreign currency facility to change five single Scots £1 notes for a Bank of England £5 note. This he immediately put into a registered envelope which he then took to a nearby post office and dispatched it to Germany. It was his Christmas present to his parents.

On the following day, Wednesday, Slater received his settlement from the Post Office Savings Bank closing his account and with the money in his pocket he called at the offices of the travel company, Thomas Cook & Sons. His mind now was firmly made up to travel by the Lusitania for he had that morning received a letter from his fellow pimp in London, Freedman, that Mrs Freedman and another girl would arrive in Glasgow on Friday morning to take over the flat as arranged. It was fairly late in the afternoon and Cook's had to contact the Cunard offices in Liverpool. The clerk told Slater that he would write to Cunard and that he was confident of a reply the following day.

It should by now be fairly clear as to what Slater was up to in his attempt to purchase a passage to America. Cook could have phoned Liverpool but the cost of the call would have added to Slater's bill. Instead, to save the money, Slater was prepared to wait until the next day. It was in Slater's interests to delay for there were plenty of ships crossing the Atlantic and as it was winter all of them had spare cabins. If the traveller was prepared to hold out he could possibly be given a reduction. What Slater was looking for is what we would now call a standby fare and they were available.

On Thursday Slater received a cheque for his Government bonds which he was cashing in. He also called back to Cook's, where the clerk told him that he had received a telegram from Liverpool offering a two berth inboard cabin for Slater and his wife, at a price of £28. Slater told the clerk that he was not interested in an inboard cabin and that instead he would travel down to Liverpool and purchase his tickets there.

Christmas day for most of Glasgow was just another working day. The banks and some of the Government offices were closed but the rest of Glasgow was at work. Scotland at that time would have no truck with such papist celebrations as Christmas.

Mrs Freedman and her colleagues had travelled up by the day train from London on the Thursday and had spent the night in the Bath Hotel. It seems that the two girls had not wasted any time for when Catherine Schmalz called to collect them on Christmas morning they were both in bed sleeping.

Originally it had been Slater's intention to leave Andree behind when he left for America but Andree had started crying and Slater had relented. The maid Catherine had been offered the choice if she wished of staying on with the two new girls, but the maid, who knew Mrs Freedman, elected to return to London and to make her own future.

Late that afternoon Slater went to the Central Station and arranged with a porter to call at the flat and collect the luggage. The porter and his mate called at 8pm and after they had left Slater, Andree and the maid took a cab to the station. The maid was going to see them off. At the station Slater purchased two third class single tickets to Liverpool on the 9.05pm train to London. The last two carriages of this train only went as far as Wigan where they were uncoupled and then continued their separate way to Liverpool. There was the usual last minute hassel, excess baggage to pay for, but they had left themselves plenty of time.

CHAPTER 10

That Friday had been an important day for Superintendent Ord for he had now become the officer in charge of the investigation into the murder of Marion Gilchrist. One of his first tasks was to issue a description of two men wanted in connection with the murder:—

(First) A man from twenty-five to thirty years of age, 5 feet 7 or 8 inches in height, thought to be clean shaven; wore a long grey overcoat and dark cap.

(Second) A man from twenty-eight to thirty years of age, tall and thin, clean shaven, nose slightly turned to one side (thought to be right side); wore a fawn-coloured overcoat (believed to be waterproof), dark trousers, tweed cloth hat of latest make, and believed to be dark in colour, and brown boots.

This notice was circulated to all police forces and with the agreement of the Chief Constable was also issued to the press. It appeared later that day in the Glasgow evening newspapers.

The fact that the descriptions of two men were issued does not necessarily mean that Ord believed that two men were involved. The first description is the one given by Arthur Adams and the second the description allegedly given by Mary Barrowman. Frankly the police were still undecided as to the number of men involved and so they decided to take no chances.

All in all it had been a fairly humdrum sort of day for Ord and at six o'clock that night, the case not having advanced at all, the Superintendent must have been contemplating calling it a day when Allan McLean walked into the police office:—

"A friend of mine had been offered a pawn ticket of a diamond brooch at the Sloper Club, and when I saw in the papers about the murder I thought that the brooch corresponded with the one for which the ticket had been offered for sale. It had been offered by a man called Oscar to my friend. When I saw the description in the paper I thought that he was the man."

McLean gave his occupation as a bicycle dealer but in fact he was a small time gambler and crook and more than probably a paid police informer as well. The fact that the police paid any attention to his rather threadbare story is proof enough of that. As McLean freely admitted, nay insisted, he had never actually spoken to the man called Oscar, indeed he was not quite sure whether Oscar was the man's first name or second name. Now there had been two descriptions published that afternoon in the papers, true neither was a very good description but they were sufficiently divergent as to be different. So which description was it that matched the man known as Oscar? On this point McLean is remarkably silent. Then again the brooch had been common knowledge since the evening of the murder so why had it taken so long for McLean's sense of civic duty to come to the surface? For that matter why had the unnamed friend, who obviously knew more about it, not come forward?

McLean told Ord that while he knew little about the man Oscar he did know where he stayed. One night, by chance, he had followed the man Oscar and another man home and he had seen Oscar enter No 69 St Georges Road. This he assumed was where Oscar stayed. On this piece of slender evidence Ord instructed a Detective Powell to go with McLean to the address and check it out. As it happened Powell knew a Mrs Bernstein who also stayed at the address and instead of checking each house in the close Powell only spoke to Bernstein. Naturally both she and her maid had never heard of the name Oscar and this seemed to content the detective for he returned to his office to report a blank.

In the mean time Ord seems to have been making enquiries of his own and it is known that detectives later that night visited the Sloper Club to make further inquiries. At midnight Ord once more instructed Powell, this time with two other detectives, to return to 69 St Georges Road and this time he was to seek an interview with a man known as Anderson.

John Trench would later argue that had Powell properly carried out his earlier assignment then Oscar Slater would never have been anything more than a brief suspect and he was probably right. As it was from midnight of the 25th, as a result of some unfortunate coincidences, Oscar Slater had become irrevocably a part of the Marion Gilchrist murder mystery.

Catherine Schmalz opened the door to Powell and his two colleagues and being a girl who was well used to being raided by the police her first reaction was to lie. No man called Anderson stayed at the address, only herself and her mistress. And where was her mistress? "Gone to Monte Carlo for Christmas", she answered defiantly.

The detectives started to search the flat and in the bedroom among some packing paper which littered the floor the remains of a piece of wrapping paper bearing the name of Oscar Slater and the address in St Georges Road was found. It was the wrapping from the small parcel sent by Dent the watchmaker containing Slater's watch. The best that Catherine could now manage was that Slater was a friend of her mistress and that the couple had left earlier in the evening for London.

The search now switched to Central Station and it was discovered that Slater and his girlfriend had boarded the 9.05 train. In those days the booking clerk was required to record every ticket he sold listing the class and destination. According to the records two single third class tickets to London had been sold for the 9.05, but so also had two single third class tickets sold for Liverpool. The porter who had brought the luggage from the flat to the station was also interviewed. With the small number of travellers that night due to Christmas he had no difficulty in recalling Slater. According to the porter the luggage had been labelled for Liverpool and he had placed the luggage in the guard's van of the Liverpool section. Thus irrespective of where Slater might have been going his luggage was bound for Liverpool.

With all the signs clearly pointing to Slater having

gone to Liverpool, Superintendent Ord for some inexplicable reason decided that Slater had gone to London. As a consequence of this decision the London police, and only the London police, were particularly asked to mount a search for Slater.

In the twelve hours following the raid on Slater's flat everybody who knew Slater was called in for questioning. Hugh Cameron, Slater's friend, was the first to be so questioned. He was hauled out of his bed in the early hours of the morning and taken to the Central police station. From Cameron, Ord found out the name of the pawnbroker with whom Slater had pledged the diamond brooch. Thus by nine o'clock on the morning of the 26th Ord knew that the brooch which Slater had pawned had absolutely nothing to do with Miss Gilchrist and that it had been pawned more than six weeks before the old lady had been murdered.

By now the police had established contact with several people who had known Slater well during his short stay in the city. Of course in those days there was no such thing as the identity-kit method of constructing a reasonable portrait of a suspect purely from verbal descriptions. But there was an alternate method which was just as good. Every large police force retained the services of a skilled artist who could reproduce a face from a description. It is hardly possible then that the Glasgow police, one of the largest forces in the country, did not have the services of such a man or that they failed to use him in such an important investigation. And yet later the police would claim that they had not taken this elementary step.

At 3.40am the two carriages from Glasgow arrived at Lime Street station in Liverpool where the only two passengers from Glasgow, a man and a woman, were met by James Dustin, the station representative of the Cunard Shipping Company. Dustin's job was to meet and assist any passengers who were travelling on with the company. Dustin directed the two travellers to the L. & N.W. hotel who had an arrangement with the shipping company and arranged for a porter to carry the luggage.

Joseph Doran was the night porter at the hotel and he clearly remembered the man and woman arriving. The couple took a double room and the man signed the register in the name of Oscar Slater, giving his point of departure as Glasgow. The next morning the guest received the bill made out in the name of Slater. Other members of the hotel staff also remembered the couple whom they also knew as Slater.

On the morning after his arrival Slater went along to the offices of the Cunard Company where he booked a second class outside cabin for two under the name of Otto Sando and wife. Before he was issued with his ticket he filled out the statutory form required in those days for all intending travellers to America.

Name	Mr Otto Sando Mrs Anny Sando
Age	38 27
Married or single	Married "
Occupation	Dentist
Country of Birth	Germany England
Last Legal residence	Scotland Scotland
Country claiming allegiance	U.S.A. U.S.A.
Final destination	Chicago Chicago
If in possession of $50 or more	Yes
If ever in United States before	Yes
No. of pieces of luggage	9

The fact that Slater had changed his name was really of little importance, certainly it was not apparently against the U.S. law for they made no demand that impending travellers use their proper names. In any case Slater was being pursued by a determined wife and it was understandable that he had no desire to make her pursuit as easy as possible.

Superintendent Duckworth of the Liverpool police had not been particularly asked to conduct a search for Slater but he had received the normal police notice regarding the fugitive. On Sunday the 27th, apparently having nothing better to do, he started his own inquiry and in the space of a couple of hours had solved the mystery of the vanishing Slater. He immediately got in touch by telephone to Glasgow to tell them that their man was at that moment on the high seas heading for New York under the name Sando.

The press had picked up the story of the raid on Slater's flat just in time for the late editions of Saturday's issues and of necessity they had only the bare bones of the story. For the Monday editions they had the whole story and it was given prominence. There was no mention, however, of the fact that the police already knew precisely where Slater was at that particular moment. As far as the press was concerned all ports were being watched for the fugitive.

On board the Lusitania as she ploughed her way through the winter storms Slater was quite unaware of the reception that was being prepared for him when he arrived in America. Like most of the other passengers Slater probably waited-up to welcome in the New Year and to hear the ship's bell announce mid-night with its sixteen chimes instead of the usual eight. With the others he more than likely raised his glass to 1909. It is to be hoped that he enjoyed himself for it was going to be a long time before he would have the opportunity to attend another New Year party.

In the early hours of the morning of January 2 just as the ship passed Sandy Hook the pilot came on board accompanied by two detectives of the New York police. Slater was wakened up and placed under arrest.

CHAPTER 11

If the Glasgow newspapers were correctly reflecting the feelings of their readers, and I suspect that they were, then Glasgow was ecstatic when the arrest of Oscar Slater was announced. Not without some glee the papers reported how, on his arrival in America, Slater had been placed in the notorious Tombs Prison in New York City and that the woman who had been travelling with him as his wife was being held by the American immigration pending a deportation hearing. As far as Glasgow was concerned at that moment it was only a matter of observing the formalities before Slater would be brought back, tried and hanged. There was, however, one tiny fly in the ointment and it is to the credit of the Glasgow Herald that they spotted it. There was a possible problem concerning the nationality of the fugitive. In New York Slater was claiming to be an American citizen which might or might not be true. But if it was untrue then undoubtedly Slater was still a German citizen so that another country, Germany, had an interest in any extradition proceedings which might be instituted and Germany of late had not been envincing any great friendship towards Great Britain. Even worse, Germany had a bigger American population than Britain.

There now followed over the next few days a series of stories which even at the time must have been known to be wildly untrue and which seems to have been planted on the press by the police. On the 5th there was a story that further arrests could be expected. On the 8th this story had been expanded to claim that the coming arrests were the result of a confession but by whom the papers did not know. Robbery was now quite definitely the motive for the murder but it was robbery with a new twist. A tray of uncut diamonds had allegedly been found worth thousands of pound sterling in the corner of a room in the dead woman's flat. This story would give rise to the widely believed rumour that Miss

Gilchrist had been a well known fence or receiver of stolen goods. The rumour was unfortunately only one of many rumours concerning the dead woman.

On the 9th there was further talk of more arrests and an unidentified policeman was quoted as saying that, "we are not resting on our oars." After this quote positively identifying the source as the police the Chief Constable issued an order that no policeman was to discuss the case with the press. This ban was greatly resented for the wrong reasons and the Daily Record struck back with an editorial:—

"The desire of the public to be kept in touch with the succession of facts that are being gradually brought to light in the investigation is quite natural. An unwritten right exists in connection with such cases that so threaten the communal sense of the reading masses to be kept apace with the gradual process of solving baffling crime. Unfortunately in this case the press had been reduced to the consideration of multitudinous rumour."

He could have gone on to point out that the source of all the *multitudinous rumour* were the police themselves.

A very popular newspaper at that time was the Scottish Weekly Record, it sold well among the less well educated. One of the star writers of this journal was a gentleman who wrote under the name of Donald Clyde and his forte was to write a weekly story based on crime. Such works of fiction were very popular with the readers. The story that appeared on January 13, as fictional as all the others, was to prove to have a long life in front of it.

In Clyde's tale there is a wealthy old woman with an ner' dowell nephew who expects to do well should the old lady die. One evening he calls on his aunt unexpectedly and surprises a burglar in the act of robbing the house. The burglar flees, carrying with him a single jewel. The nephew, realising the opportunity, murders the aunt and blames the crime on the burglar. Of course Clyde made no pretence that his story was anything other than fiction but his readers, used to him solving baffling crime every week, seems to have assumed that he had some inside information. In the years that followed the crime elements of Clyde's story would surface from time to time as being fact.

Clyde's story appeared on the 13th and by the following day the Gilchrist murder had, for the time being, become a dead story. The attention of the readers of the newspapers was now directed towards a juicy divorce case that was just starting at the High Court. An officer of the Guards was suing his wife for divorce on the grounds of adultery with a member of the Scottish Aristocracy. As the husband had caught his wife and her lover in the very act of congress, they were at it on a sofa in the library and hadn't even bothered to take the precaution of locking the door, the story promised to do well for circulation.

As a last act of acknowledgement to the Gilchrist murder on the 14th the papers published a photograph of Oscar Slater. Who supplied the photograph was never revealed but as it was carried by all of the papers then the police look suspiciously like the source. But whatever its origins it did ensure that from that day on everybody knew what like Slater looked.

CHAPTER 12

Because there existed an Extradition Treaty between the Government of Great Britain and the United States it was possible for his Brittanic Majesty to request the return of Oscar Slater to Scotland to face grave charges against the laws of that country as specified by the Lord Advocate. To secure the extradition, however, it was going to take a lot more than just a piece of paper and the Lord Advocate's say so.

One area of difficulty lay in the difference of attitude towards the interpretation of the treaty. England tending to be more ready to observe the spirit while America tended to stick more readily to the strict letter. The treaty clearly required the requesting Government to produce sufficient *prima facie* evidence to show that they had a case to go before a jury and were not just hoping that once they had their hands on the prisoner they would secure a confession. This requirement was totally at varience with the Scottish practice where the evidence is only made public at the trial.

The man charged with preparing the evidence against Oscar Slater was the Procurator-fiscal, James Neill Hart. Half a century before his father had been the Procurator-fiscal at the time of the trial of Madeleine Smith and he had played a leading role in manufacturing the evidence against her. James was to prove to be a worthy son of his father.

The problem facing Hart was that at the time when he had to make the application for extradition, sometime between December 28 and January 1, he had no evidence against Slater except his three eye-witnesses and of course Helen was claiming that she had never really had a good look at the stranger in the hall. However, luckily, when she was approached afresh she was found to be quite prepared to modify her original statement. Indeed she gave the Procurator-fiscal a choice of stories. From her original claim that she had been standing at the entrance of the short lobby leading to the kitchen when the stranger had appeared out from the bedroom she was now prepared to admit to having been in the middle of the hall. Thus from saying that all she had seen was the man's face in profile for a split second she had now moved to having seen the man's face full frontal.

While this was a decided improvement Hart obviously thought that Helen could be persuaded to do better and Helen was more than willing to oblige. She now modified her statement again to say that she had in fact been standing just in front of Arthur Adams when the man had appeared. Even better she now claimed that while Arthur had been rooted to the spot she had turned and watched the man until he had vanished from sight down the stairs. Thus she had a longer view of the stranger and as such was the better witness. James Hart, like his father before him, must have thought himself to be a very clever chap indeed.

The moment that it became known that Slater proposed to contest the application decisions had to be taken as to who should be sent to America. Hart decided, and he really had no other choice, that Helen Lambie, Mary Barrowman and Arthur Adams should go. Documents, such as the autopsy reports and certain of the precognitions would also be required and this would require someone to accompany them in order to swear to their authenticity. For this an official of the court would be necessary and William Warnock, a Sheriff's Criminal Officer, was chosen. In charge of the party, and of the prisoner should the application be successful, was Inspector Pyper.

The departure of the party from Glasgow to Liverpool where they were to board the SS Baltic for the Atlantic crossing was shrouded in secrecy. On January 14 an enterprising reporter from the Daily Record was hanging around Central Station when he spotted Warnock and Pyper boarding the Liverpool train. When he checked with police Headquarters he was told that they knew nothing about it. Either he had missed the other three or they had travelled by another train.

The North Atlantic in January is normally a wild place and 1909 was no exception. The SS Baltic was so delayed by storms that instead of the normal eight days for the crossing, they had been sent by one of the slower boats, the trip took twelve days. Adams and Warnock proved to be bad sailors and spent most of the time in their cabin. Mary Barrowman was really nothing more than a child with no experience of either being in the company of adults or of dining with strangers. She too spent most of the voyage in her cabin. Helen Lambie and Inspector Pyper on the other hand were of the stuff of sailors and so they quite enjoyed the trip.

CHAPTER 13

In New York Slater was among friends who could advise him and he had more than sufficient money with which to hire himself a good lawyer. He had a deposit still with a New York bank. The lawyers he turned to, and it is hard to see where he could have done better, was Hugh Gordon Miller assisted by William Goodhart. Miller was a shrewd, cracker-barrel, Connecticut Yankee, the very model for an American defence lawyer of the type so successfully played by such actors as Spencer Tracy and James Stewart.

The extradition hearing had been scheduled to take place before Commissioner Shield on January 23 but because of the gales the witnesses did not even arrive in New York until the 25th. From the boat the three witnesses, Helen, Arthur and Mary, were taken direct to the office of attorney, Charles Fox, who had been retained by the British Government to act as their representative at the hearing. Fox spent what little time he had before the hearing commenced on the morning of the 26th in rehearsing his witnesses. Among other things he showed each witness a recent photograph of Oscar Slater. Even after being shown the photograph several times Mary Barrowman still had difficulty in recognising him.

The hearing took place in the Immigration Building and although not a court room it was arranged as though it was one. The Commissioner sat at a raised desk with his clerk and stenographer in front and slightly below. The two sets of attorneys sat at separate desks facing the Commissioner and the witness under examination. The spectators were separated from the well of the court by a low wooden barrier. We are all familiar enough with American court procedure from the films and television to recognise the layout. The room was very small, much too small, for the crowd of reporters who occupied the public area. The crowded conditions were made even worse by the fact that no public seating was provided and that smoking was permitted.

The room was situated at the end of a short corridor and while waiting for the proceeding to start Helen, Mary and Inspector Pyper remained in the corridor. As they were standing there Oscar Slater was led-by handcuffed to a 6ft-6 inch giant of a U.S. Marshal.

The first witness to be called to the stand was William Warnock and ordinarily, as his task was solely to authenticate the documents in the case, his appearance on the witness stand should have been a formality, but Miller had other ideas. Perhaps he hoped that by giving Warnock a rough ride he could prevoke a feeling of apprehension in the other witnesses, especially the two girls. On the other hand, perhaps he was merely ensuring good copy for the reporters present.

Miller affected a great interest in the form of the legal system in Scotland, an interest not shared by the Commissioner. Leaning forward Shield reminded the attorney that because of the weather the hearing had been delayed and as a consequence the calendar was now overcrowded. "Are you not interested in how another legal system works?" demanded Miller. "Not really,' replied the Commissioner resignedly, "but I fear that I am going to learn anyway."

In point of fact, irrespective of what the Commissioner thought, Miller was perfectly right. It was an important section of the Extradition Treaty that all the evidence being offered to the hearing had been secured in a manner acceptable to American legal practice.

Step by step Miller took the luckless Warnock through the minutiae of the Scottish system as he understood it and as the number of questions increased Warnock unfortunately tended to become more pompous. The titles especially seemed to tickle the attorney's fancy and at one stage he took to calling Warnock 'The Lord High Marshal of Glasgow'. At another point he demanded to know whether a sheriff in Scotland carried a gun. When Warnock replied that they did not, Miller claimed triumphantly, "well ours do." All good knock about Republican stuff designed to capture the attention of the press.

Charles Fox now called Helen Lambie to the stand and quickly took her through her evidence. "Do you now see the man that you saw in the hall that night in this room?" In the best approved manner Helen carefully glanced about the room before looking directly at the table where everybody knew that Slater would be sitting. At the table Goodhart rose and placed himself in the direct line of her vision but by half-rising Helen was able to see round him. "That is the man there," she said, pointing directly at Slater.

Miller now rose to cross-examine and carefully he took her through the various statements she had made in Glasgow as to precisely where she had been standing in thc hall when the stranger had appeared. Helen was forced to admit that she had made contradictory statements:—

Miller:—Well then which of these statements are we to believe?—No answer.

You see the position that we are in, don't you? You have so far given three versions. Firstly, you claimed that as you were standing at the entrance to the lobby then you had only the briefest glimpse of the man's face. In your second statement you claim that you were in the middle of the hall. If this is true then at best you only saw the man's face for as long as it took him to walk two or three steps. In your third statement you claim that you were standing by the outside door but even there you did not see the man's face for any length of time and, presumably, the man was doing his best not to be recognised?—

Miller continued without waiting for an answer.

Miller:—Prior to the start of this hearing were you standing in the corridor outside this room?—Yes.

Did you see the United States Marshal bringing in the prisoner?—I saw the prisoner.

The Marshal is a pretty big man, he is well over six feet tall. Did you not notice him?—No.

He is very broad?—No.

He is a regular giant of a man?—I only noticed the prisoner.
As the marshal with his prisoner handcuffed to him passed you by did the man standing with you say, "there is the man you have come to identify"?—No, I said to Inspector Pyper, "there is the man."
Yesterday, when you arrived in New York, did you meet with Mr Fox in his office?—Yes.
Did he show you a photograph of Mr Slater?—He showed me a number of photographs of which the prisoner was one.
But you did see a photograph of Mr Slater?—Yes.
And that is why you were able to recognise him in the corridor?—No, I recognised him by his walk.
His walk?—Yes, he had a very peculiar walk. It is by his walk that I remember him from Glasgow.

Now this was something entirely new for at no time had any suggestion of a peculiar walk ever been mentioned until that moment. After much discussion as to the nature of the peculiarity Helen was invited to step down and demonstrate that which she was finding difficulty to put into words. As this entailed the lifting of her skirt to show the feet the reporters present were entertained to the sight of a well turned Scottish ankle. The Commissioner was shocked but, apart from the thrill, the walk was not particularly impressive.

Miller now turned to a more detailed examination of the flat occupied by Miss Gilchrist and her maid:—
Miller:—It is a pretty big flat?—Six rooms and a kitchen.
By New York standards I would say that that is a pretty big flat?—They are quite common in Glasgow.
Now what is this hall that has been mentioned?—It is something similar to a corridor.
You mean that all the rooms open on to the hall?—Yes.
So that when you first enter the flat it is into the hall?—Yes.
In New York most of the front doors open directly into the living-room. Are there such flats in Glasgow—Yes,

the poor people stay in them.
Well I am not exactly wealthy but I would not describe myself as being poor.

Amid the general laughter a rueful Miller indicated that he was finished with Helen, at least for the moment.

Helen had been under pressure for more than two hours during the questioning and the fact that she could still put down a man of Miller's statue speaks volumes for her quickness of mind. Helen was a lot smarter than was generally appreciated and this was not lost on Gordon Miller. But then he was no fool himself.

Mary Bannerman was now called by Fox and when she came to the crucial point she had no difficulty in pointing out Oscar Slater as being the man who had allegedly bumped into her outside the close on the night of Miss Gilchrist's death. Having done what was required of her Mary was now turned over to Miller for cross-examination. In light of her tender years the attorney elected to take the avuncular approach:—
Miller:—Well then Mary, did you enjoy your boat-trip?—No Sir. It was very rough and I was sick.
So you spent a great deal of your time in your cabin?—Yes Sir.
I understand that you shared a cabin with the other witness, Helen Lambie?—Yes Sir.
Tell me, did you and Miss Lambie, while you were alone, did you ever discuss the reason why you were coming to America?—Oh no Sir!
Come Mary, you were on the boat together for twelve days and for a deal of that time you were together, alone, in your cabin. Are you seriously saying that you never once discussed the reason why you were on a ship coming to New York?—No Sir, before we left we were told that we were not to speak about it.

Miller had made a bad start to his cross-examination for he automatically assumed—years ago as a young man reading about the Oscar Slater case for the first time I made the same assumption, as did many others—some degree of collusion when his common sense should have told him different. One of the surprises that I met with when researching this book was the bitterness exhibited by Mary about her treatment on the ship by Helen. Far from talking about the case Helen hardly spoke a dozen words to Mary during the twelve days of the voyage.

In truth Helen had a number of good reasons for not talking to Mary about the case and indeed for avoiding her company altogether. In fact Helen probably discussed the case extensively during the voyage but not with Mary. Both she and Inspector Pyper proved to be good sailors and they were in each others company almost exclusively during the trip.

Miller decided on another track:—

Miller:—That is a nice coat you are wearing. Did you get it to come to America?—Yes Sir.

Did you get many new clothes?—Yes Sir.

And who helped you buy the clothes?—My mother, Sir.

I see. You chose the clothes and your mother paid for them?—No Sir. My mother helped be choose but Mr Pyper paid for them.

Inspector Pyper had not actually paid for the clothes, they were paid for out of the contingency fund and very properly too. To have sent Mary to America in her own clothes would have been an insult both to the girl and to Glasgow. I have no doubt that but for the contingency fund some public minded citizen would have stepped in to prevent an embarrassment. But was it absolutely necessary for a police inspector to be so closely identified with the buying of the clothes, especially the inspector in charge of the investigation? If they could not trust Mrs Barrowman then why did they not seek the help of the wife of a senior officer? The whole episode smacks strongly of what Miller was seeking to suggest, that the witness had been bought.

Miller now turned to the incident that had allegedly taken place in the corridor before the hearing had commenced when Slater had been led by in handcuffs.

Mary, like Helen, denied that Pyper had been the author of the disputed remark and again, like Helen, she claimed the honour of saying, "there is the man we have come to identify." But in fact, although much is usually made of the incident, the whole thing was something of a red herring for it did not really matter who said the offending words, if indeed they ever were uttered. The day before both the witnesses had been shown a photograph of Slater at the office of Mr Fox and after that anything else could only be re-inforcement.

Having been brought over the Atlantic at some expense and after having been shown the photograph of Slater the most that Arthur Adams was prepared to say was that Slater looked something like the stranger in the hall. He would not go any further than this on the grounds that it was, "too serious a matter for an easy judgement." As to where Helen was standing when the stranger had appeared in the hall Arthur had no doubs, Helen had been wrong in what she claimed. Having said this he readily conceeded that it threw some doubt on the accuracy of Helen's identification.

Arthur's evidence finished the hearing for that day and because of other commitments Commissioner Shield was not available for the following day so that the hearing was adjourned for two days. In this case, however, justice delayed was not justice denied. The delay allowed more time for the story to reach more of the German and Jewish communities scattered over America.

CHAPTER 14

When the hearing resumed on the 28th, Commissioner Shield confidently expected that it would be the final day but he was mistaken. Miller dropped something of a bombshell by requesting that he should be allowed to recall Helen Lambie to the witness-stand. He wasted little time on preliminaries:—

Miller:—Do you know a man called Patrick Nugent?—Yes.

What is your relationship with Nugent?—We are friends.

Have you known him long?—About a year.

What does this man Nugent do for a living?—I am not quite sure.

Is it not a fact that he is a bookmaker?—I believe that he is.

So he is a gambler. Where did you meet this gambler?—At a dance at Wishaw. That is a small town near Glasgow.

When did you meet him for the first time?—A year ago, it was at a New Year's dance.

And you started to walk out with him?—No. just on a few occasions.

And on these occasions where did you go, to church?—No.

Did you introduce this gambler to your mistress?—Yes, once. He came to see me when we were on holiday and Miss Gilchrist invited him to dine with her.

And how did you desribe this gambler to your mistress?—I told her that he was a coal-miner.

Did this gambler ever call at your mistress's flat?—Yes, he came to tea on one occasion.

Was your mistress present?—No, she was away from home.

Did you show this gambler some of the jewellery owned by your mistress?—No, but I believe that I mentioned that my mistress was a wealthy woman. I wanted to impress him.

Did you show this gambler the various rooms of the flat?—Yes.

In the moral climate prevailing at that time both in America and Britain a gambler was regarded as being little better than a common criminal. Indeed the police treated them as being the same hence the standard allegation that a person was suspect merely for being an associate of criminals and gamblers. Thus on one level simply by showing that Helen was a friend of a gambler Miller was challenging the credibility of Helen as a witness.

But on another level Miller was going much further than this for by raising the visit of Nugent to the flat while the mistress was absent he was also suggesting that Nugent should be regarded with suspicion. And if Nugent was a suitable candidate for suspicion then Helen herself could not be above suspicion.

It is interesting to speculate just where Miller got his intimate knowledge of Helen's private life from, and how he discovered that Nugent was a bookie. A number of documents, particularly some of the precognitions, had been sent to New York as part and parcel of the case for extradition but whether Nugent's precognition was included must be doubtful. Nugent's presence in the case was only as a peripheral witness and nothing in his precognition suggests that he was being regarded as a suspect. Curiously enough as part of the precognition Nugent was required to give his job or profession and this appear as being a Commission Agent which of course he was not, a fact which must have been known to the person conducting the precognition. A Commission Agent was a legal book-maker while a street bookie was wholly illegal.

Miller continued his explanation:—

Miller:—Two days ago when you were giving evidence you told us that the outside door to the flat and the door to what you called the close were fitted with locks?—That is correct.

Could the door to the close be opened without a key?—From the inside, yes. From the outside, no. It could only

be opened by a check key.
How many locks were fitted to the door of the flat?—Three.
Did all these locks require a key?—It depends whether you were outside or inside. If you were inside you could open the Yale lock without a key but if you were outside then you needed a key for all the locks.
So that if you were standing in the street and you wanted to get into the flat you would require four keys?—Yes.
Were these four keys kept separate or together?—Together. They were tied together by a piece of string.
Was this the only set of keys?—As far as I am aware of.
And you were in the employment of Miss Gilchrist for three years before her death?—Yes.
You are aware of the police statement that all of the windows were securely locked and that there was no sign of a forced entry?—Yes.
When you left the flat that evening how did you secure the door?—I pulled the door shut on the Yale lock and turned the key in the Chubb.
So how do you suppose that the stranger got into the house?—I suppose that Miss Gilchrist admitted him.

But that was the point. If Helen had in her possession the only set of keys to the flat then Miss Gilchrist could not have admitted anybody to the house.

For the remainder of that day Miller produced a series of witnesses who all spoke of Slater's honesty. These witnesses were all Jewish and connected with the jewellery trade. Each claimed that from time to time Slater had acted as their British agent, they would send him stones, usually emeralds, which he would sell and transmit the money, less commission, back to America. They had always found him honest.

When the hearing adjourned that day the Commissioner intimated that he would hear the final submissions on the following day, that is on January 29. In fact it would be February 6 before the hearing would be resumed and without any official explanation as to the reason for the delay.

On the morning of the 6th Miller rose to address the hearing. His client, he claimed, had every confidence that extradition would be denied and that in a few short hours he would be a free man. However, such a freedom could only be conditional for many would still suspect that he had indeed been involved in the murder of Miss Gilchrist. Thus his client, if he accepted the due process of the law, would be condemned to live out the remainder of his life under a cloud. This his client considered to be intollerable and so he had decided, against the advice of his advisers, to withdraw his opposition to extradition, choosing instead to return to Scotland where he confidently expected to be cleared of the charge. He showed a rare if misguided trust in Scottish justice.

Miller was right when he claimed that he was confident that extradition would be denied and not only because of the evidence he had submitted. There was a good chance that both the American and British Governments had blundered.

The British Government had applied for extradition while Slater had, in fact, still been in their jurisdiction, he had been on a British ship sailing in international waters. The proper course for the British Government should have been to have instructed the master of the ship to place Slater in detention until the ship returned to British waters.

The American Government had also slipped up by permitting two members of the New York police to board the ship, place Slater under arrest, and then take him into America whether he wished to go there or not. The correct procedure should have been for the police to have waited until Slater actually put his foot on American soil before arresting him. This is precisely what they did in the case of Slater's travelling companion.

Interestingly enough forty years after Slater the British Government, at the request of America, boarded a Polish ship at Southampton and arrested a German called Eisler on an extradition warrant. When the case came to court it was thrown out on the grounds that Eisler had made no attempt to set foot in Britain.

There were however factors apart from the legal position which was worrying the American Government. As Slater was a German citizen, albeit one who was wanted for avoiding conscription, the German Government was also interested in the case and it was probably the international wrangle between the three Governments that was the cause the long delay to the hearing.

With little evidence to support it, I strongly suspect that representatives of the British Government got to Slater in the Tombs prison where he was being held and did a deal with him. I suspect that the deal was that if Slater voluntarily returned he was promised that he would be quickly freed and suitably compensated.

Miller was a good lawyer who firmly believed in the innocence of his client. As such he must have warned Slater that to return without some kind of guarantee would be to place his head in the noose. He must also have told him that even if he was extradited his departure could be delayed for years while the case worked its way through the appeal courts. Slater had everything to gain by sitting tight and everything to lose by giving up.

I have three reasons for making my allegation for a deal having been made. Firstly, as we shall see shortly, there is the reaction of Slater following his remand in Glasgow. Secondly, in spite of the complete lack of any mitigating circumstances Slater did not hang. Thirdly, and perhaps most importantly, all the records concerning the extradition application have become a state secret of such magnitude that they have been locked away until well into the next century. I think that I may say without fear of contradiction that such a restriction is unparalleled in any other murder investigation.

The day after Helen had given her evidence for the second time she and Arthur Adams returned to

Glasgow, they had been in New York for all of four days. Mary Barrowman was the next to leave. She had been allowed to stay longer for she had relatives in New York. Finally, on the 14th, Pyper, Warnock and Slater sailed on the SS Columbia direct for the Clyde. It seems to have been an easier crossing for the trip took only seven days. In order to avoid any disturbance, their arrival was expected and there was a crowd at the docks, all three men disembarked at Renfrew, a small town some miles down river from Glasgow. Among the welcoming party who greeted them when they came ashore was Detective Constable Trench, armed with the official warrant for arrest.

Oscar Slater

CHAPTER 15

Much would be made at the trial of Oscar Slater by certain witnesses of Slater's foreign looks and it is worthwhile at this point to consider just how foreign looking he actually was. Slater had a good head of black or dark hair and the centre of his face was dominated by a luxurient, black moustache of the type favoured by military men. This then had the undoubted effect of making the whole face slightly dark in appearance. But in Scotland, even today, most males have dark hair and in 1909 the heavy military type of moustache was very popular. As can be seen from the 1908 photograph his features have none of the characteristics popularly believed to be typical of people of jewish origin. In truth Slater had not the kind of face that particularly stood out in a crowd.

Where Slater did differ from the man in the Glasgow street was in the clothes he wore. At that time, through the good offices of the Co-operative Society, most working men had one good suit, usually kept for occasions such as weddings and funerals. This suit was invariably made from a dark blue, serge cloth, double-breasted and with the jacket cut short. So common was the suit that one could be pardoned for believing that somewhere in England there existed a gigantic factory dedicated to clothing the working men of Scotland. This ensemble was usually completed by a bowler hat (tradesmen and only then on the most formal of occasions) or a bunnet and worn with either a shirt and tie or a scarf. Black boots were a must.

The middle-class were a bit more adventurous as befits those with more than a one suit wardrobe. But even here most suits were always of a dark, heavy worsted or tweed. Shirts were dark shades, and made of poplin, a cotton cloth invented in Scotland and used as a cheap substitute for linen.

Slater's wardrobe, as a result of his travels, had been collected from all over the place; London, Paris, New

York. His mode of dress was truely international. He also had an amazing amount of clothes by the standards of the day. Six or seven suits, all of good quality. Among his numerous shirts he had six which had cost no less than 16/11d each, as he so informed the laundry when they lost one temporarily. As a punishment for their carelessness he refused to pay. And this at a time when captains of industry in Glasgow would cavil at paying more than 5/-d for a shirt.

Slater in the street would have been instantly recognisable as being not of the city by his mode of dress. In a line-up with eleven others chosen at random Slater would have been about as inconspicuous as a Highlander in national costume in a London identity parade.

From the ship Slater was taken direct to the Central police office and almost immediately he took part in the first of a number of identification parades. In fairness it has to be said that certain steps were taken in order to ensure an unbiased identification. Great care was taken to make sure that no witness could catch even a glimpse prior to the actual parade, However, it also has to be said that the steps taken in fact turned out to be little more than cosmetic.

The identification parade took place in a large room and it consisted of, apart from Slater, nine policemen in civilian clothes and two railway policemen, also in civilian clothes. Not all of these men were dark haired, not were they all sporting luxurient moustaches. Given the level of pay paid to policemen in those days it is unlikely that any of them could be described as being well-dressed. As at that time was a minimum height requirement of 5ft.10 inches for entry into the police then Slater must have been the smallest man in the room. And of course every witness had already seen the photograph of Slater which had been published in the newspapers and which more than likely they had cut out to keep as an aid to their memory. It is hardly surprising then that no one failed to recognise Slater.

Later that afternoon, in the presence of Trench,

Pyper and Warnock examined Slater's luggage. When he had been arrested in New York all his luggage had been impounded and sealed and as most of this luggage had travelled in the guard's van and then in the hold of the Lusitania this was the first time that much of it was seeing the light of day since it had been packed on Christmas day.

What of course Pyper was looking for were signs of blood stained clothing and a minute examination was conducted. The only suspicious items was a raincoat, light in colour, which had some dark stains on it. The hammer, which along with the other cheap tools Slater had purchased, was also found and this too was laid to one side for closer examination. Generally speaking all three men were agreed that all the signs appeared to be that the clothing had been carefully packed. If Slater had been fleeing hurriedly then his luggage did not bear this out.

Slater was charged with murder on Monday, February 13th. As is usual the hearing only lasted a couple of minutes and he was remanded to Duke Street prison. The newspapers all carried a report of the proceedings along with a curious footnote, they all reported that when Slater had been returned to his cell he had undergone some kind of hysterical breakdown. As the press had been unusually well informed about the generally more obscure details of the case then we can have no reason to doubt the accuracy of the story. It does raise the question, however, as to why a man who has already been in custody for six weeks and who had faced an extradition hearing should suddenly have a nervous breakdown at this stage of the proceedings. I suspect that the real reason was that he suddenly realised that he had been double-crossed and that the authorities intended to put him on trial.

In Scottish criminal procedure there is no committal trail such as exists in England where the prosecution has to lay out all the evidence in advance. In Scotland all the witnesses appearing for the prosecution are instead formally precognosced. In this procedure the witnesses are taken individually before a sheriff in Chambers where they are sworn before making a statement as to what they know of the matter. The statement is then written down and signed by the witness. Legally these statements are the property of the prosecution for they form the basis of the case against the accused but there is a tradition that the defence can have access to the statements should they request it. This is a courtesy apparently which is never refused by the Lord Advocate which leads one to ask the question, why then is it not made a right?

Scotland also differs from England in the amount of time allowed the prosecution in serious cases where the accused is normally held in custody without bail. At that time such cases were time barred and the accused had to be tried within 114 days of being detained. But there was also a requirement that the accused had to be served with the indictment and list of witnesses at least 28 days before the commencement of the trial and that after that date no new witnesses could be added to the list without showing cause. Thus after deducting trial time the prosecution had only some 92 days in which to prepare its case. This rule has recently been changed to read that it is now sufficient merely for the trial to begin within 114 days.

Slater had retained the services of Ewing Spiers, a Glasgow solicitor. On April 6, twenty-eight days exactly before the date set for the trial, in Duke Street prison, in the presence of his solicitor, Oscar Slater was served with the indictment:—

Oscar Slater, sometime residing at 69 St Georges Road, Glasgow, and presently a prisoner in Glasgow, you are indicted at the instance Of the Right Honourable Alexander Ure, His Majesty's Advocate, and the charge against you is that you did, on 21st December, at number 15 Queen's Terrace, West Princes Street, Glasgow, assault the said Marion Gilchrist, and beat her with a hammer or other blunt instrument, and fractured her skull, and did murder her.

T.B. Morrison, AD.

In the half century that had elapsed since the trial of Madeleine Smith the Crown Office had seemingly at least learned the virtue of brevity in drawing up indictments.

The indictment is interesting for two points. Firstly, there is no mention of any robbery and yet it is difficult to see how it could be alleged that Slater was the murderer without some reference being made to robbery. Secondly, the weapon is specified, a hammer. As we know when Slater's luggage was examined a hammer had been found, but what then of the auger which also had been thought to be the weapon? Changing weapons in the middle of an enquiry smacks of opportunism.

Fourteen days after the serving of the indictment Slater was moved from Glasgow to Edinburgh where the trial was to be held. At the Pleading Diet which preceeds the start of the session Slater pled Not Guilty although he really had no choice in the matter. In capital cases in Scotland the prisoner is not permitted to plead Guilty.

In a trial for murder the prosecution has to devide its case into three distinct elements; motive, means and opportunity, although not necessarily in that order. In spite of it not being mentioned in the indictment robbery would be advanced as the motive. The means would be the hammer found in his possession. The opportunity would be by proving that Slater was the mysterious stranger in the hall. Any rational review of the evidence at that time would have shown that the prosecution had no case.

CHAPTER 16

The trial opened at 10am on Monday morning, May 3, 1909 in the High Court in Edinburgh before Lord Guthrie. Appearing for the prosecution were Alexander Ure, Lord Advocate, T.B. Morrison, K.C. and W. Lyon, both Advocate-Depute. Appearing for the defence were A.L. McClure, K.C. and John Mair, Advocate. Without any fuss the jury were empanelled, the indictment read and the first witness called. As I have already dealt with much of the prosecution case I will tend now to deal mainly with the rebutal offered by the defence.

For a case where no robbery was being alleged the choice of the first two witnesses was perhaps surprising. David Dick, a valuator, told the court that he had prepared a valuation of the jewellery owned by the dead woman. The list contained some 57 items at a total trade value of £1,382. If bought new in a shop the value would be perhaps twice this figure. From a photograph taken from a trade journal of the missing brooch he valued it at £50.

William Sorley, a partner in the firm of R&W Sorley, Jewellers, told the court that his firm had sold the missing brooch to Miss Gilchrist. His firm also cleaned the jewellery owned by the dead woman on a regular basis and the last time he had seen the brooch was in March, 1908.

Jane Duff, housewife, was now called to the stand. In her single days she had been employed as a maid by Miss Gilchrist. She had been with her for five years, leaving to get married in 1900. When she had first taken up employment her wage had been £12 per annum rising to £16 by the time that she left. According to Jane it was common knowledge in the district that Miss Gilchrist was a wealthy woman but she hastened to assure the court that she had not told anyone. Under cross-examination she would modify her original statement.

McClure:—You said that from conversation with

people in the neighbourhood that you thought that they were aware that she had a lot of jewellery?—It was sometime remarked to me in shops while I was shopping.
What was said?—I cannot remember the words exactly except that Miss Gilchrist dressed very well and wore some jewellery.
Did she ever wear anything except a brooch and a couple of bracelets?—Not every day, except that and three rings.
And she wore gloves?—Yes.
So that the visible jewellery that this lady would carry would be two bracelets?—Yes, she was particular that her jewellery was not visible.
What leads you to say that there was a rumour that she was a wealthy lady?—I do not think that it was a very special remark, further than people speaking to me in the shop that she dressed well.

Jane Duff had been away from Miss Gilchrist for eight years so that anything as to whether her ex-mistress's wealth was public knowledge or not had to be dated.

Between Jane Duff and Helen Lambie there had been at least one other maid, Margaret Fergusion. What is more this maid had kept in contact with her mistress after she had left and therefore would have proved to be a far more knowledgeable witness but she was never called. Perhaps the fact that Mrs Fergusion and her daughter were the main beneficiaries to the fortune had something to do with it.

There now followed a number of witnesses who spoke to Slater's renting of the flat and his furnishing of it. These matters disposed of the first policeman was called.

Constable Brien, whom we have already met, remembered seeing a man about a week before the murder near to the corner of West Princes Street with St Georges Road. The man had been leaning against some railings and appeared to be drunk, otherwise there was nothing particularly suspicious about the incident. Certainly Brien had not challenged the man. At an an identity parade where nine of the men were fellow policemen he had no difficulty in picking out Oscar Slater.

Just precisely what the jury were expected to take from this evidence is not at all clear. If true then all it amounted to was that Slater was waiting until he was sober before he went home. Many of the jury could have easily identified with the feeling.

There now followed a group of four witnesses, all related, whose evidence, if true, was potentially damaging to the accused.

Mrs McHaffie lived in a first floor flat with her farrier husband and daughter across the street from Miss Gilchrist. By some judious straining of the neck it was possible for Mrs McHaffie to see into the sitting-room of the old lady. By nature, a nosey woman, Mrs McHaffie, by her own admission, spent hours at her front window watching her neighbours. There was little that happened in the street below that escaped her attention.

The story that Mrs McHaffie had to tell the court was that during the weeks before the murder, always during the day, she had seen a man on several occasions loitering on the pavement opposite. That is to say under the windows of the flat occupied by Miss Gilchrist. Although the man had never been any nearer than thirty yards and she had always been above him nevertheless she was able to give a remarkably good description. The man was dark, had a moustache, about forty years of age and not very tall. Generally he had been wearing a light overcoat, check trousers, spats and a black bowler hat.

And what had this man been doing that might have occasioned suspicion? Well not really very much. On occasions he would walk a little way up the street and then return. Sometimes he looked all around him. Even occasionally he glanced up at the window but when he saw Mrs McHaffie watching him he put down his head and moved away. In fact he seems not to have been doing much in particular.

Strangely enough in spite of her suspicions Mrs McHaffie never saw fit to tell the police while the initial investigation was taking place and the street below her window was crawling with policemen. Instead she waited until the middle of January, after Slater's description and photograph had been published in the papers, and then only after the police had called at the house.

The suspicious stranger had also been seen by Margaret McHaffie, the unmarried daughter, but she was not quite so sure that the man was Slater:—

McClure:—Were you down at the police station for purposes of identification on the same day as your mother?—Yes.

How many foreign looking people were there when you went in?—He was the only one.

And was he like the photograph you had seen?—Yes.

Had you read of his description in the papers?—Yes.

Is it your evidence that the man is like and resembles the person in West Princes Street?—No, he is the man I saw loitering in West Princes Street.

Is it not the case that you were not prepared to swear to him at first?—Yes, but I thought over what I had told the Crown, and I still adhere to what I said.

Why were you not prepared at one time to swear to his being the man?—I did not think that it was necessary at the time.

When were you not quite sure?—When I was interviewed by Mr Speirs (defence solicitor).

Can you tell us when this was?—It would be in March.

As I understand it, that would be about three months after you had seen the man in West Princes Street?—Yes.

What has made you change your mind since the middle of March?—I said to the Crown that he was the man, and I say he is the man still.

But that is not the point. Seeing that you were unable to

say in the month of March that this was the man, what has enabled you to change your mind and say now that he is the man?—I have been thinking it over, and I have come to the conclusion that he is the man I saw loitering about.
Were you at any time suspicious of him?—When I saw him loitering I wondered what he was loitering about for.
Surely you do not suspect people who merely walk up and down the street?—But seeing him so often, and at about the same time . . .
What did you suspect him of in broad daylight?—I did not suspect him. I just wondered what he was doing.
Were you suspicious of anything?—I was not suspicious of him doing anything at that time.
Might he have been waiting for a friend?—He might.
Did you see him do anything peculiar?—No.
Did you see him do anything which would lead you to suppose that he was affraid of being seen?—No.
Did you communicate with the police, or did they come to you first?—They came to us first.
How long after the murder was it that the police called on you?—I think that it was in January.

Madge McHaffie was a niece who lived nearby and who visited her aunt on a couple of occasions during December. On one of these occasions, at seven o'clock in the evening, Madge had a face to face encounter with the stranger. She was climbing the stair to her aunt's flat when she was passed by the man going down. Fortunately the stair was well lit so she was able to give a good description. He was wearing black check trousers, a fawn overcoat, a black bowler, and fawn gaiters.

Continuing up the stair Madge was admitted to her aunt's flat by Mrs McHaffie's married daughter, Annie. As she entered the house Madge mentioned seeing the man on the stair and her cousin told her that he had been at their door. He had asked whether a man called Anderson lived there and when she had told him no the man had turned on his heels and gone down stairs.

Anderson, of course, was the name that Slater was using at the time.

The raid on Slater's flat and the fact that he was using the name of Anderson had been published in all the newspapers on December 26. The photograph of Slater complete with distinctive moustache had been likewise published on January 14. The information then that the McHaffie girls were able to give the police could have been gleaned from the newspapers. What had not been published, however, was that during the weeks before the murder Slater had removed his moustache so that at the time Mrs McHaffie claims to have seen him loitering he was relatively clean shaven. Nevertheless Mrs McHaffie describes him as having a moustache. Similarly it had never been reported that Slater had a pronounced German accent and yet Annie, who claims to have spoken to the stranger, makes no mention of this obvious fact. It is difficult not to suspect conspiracy to commit perjury.

Is it a case then that the McHaffies were so wanton and lacking in any sense of responsibility that they would lie an innocent man to the gallows? Oddly enough the answer to this need not necessarily be yes.

A few years ago in England a woman was quite deliberately shot to death in the presence of her husband and family during a robbery. A man, who had a record for violence, was arrested and charged with the murder and at the trial the husband and family positively identified him as being the man who had pulled the trigger. Because the first trial had to be abandoned a second trial took place and again the family identified him. The accused however was set free after offering an alibi, he was in bed with the wife of another notorious criminal at the time. There must have been very few people in England who believed the alibi. In fact, shortly afterwards, another man was arrested for the murder and convicted.

Now, did the husband and family of the murdered woman lie when they identified the first man? No, they genuinely believed that when they identified the first man they were telling the truth. They had, for some inexplicable reason, made an error.

At around the beginning of the century in England a man called Adolph Beck was convicted on a charge of a fraud and sentenced to five years imprisonment. It was alleged that Beck had formed associations with women of a certain age and who were all possessed of a small 'nest-egg'. His technique was to insinuate marriage and thus gain possession of his victims' few pounds. At the trial ten women who had been so swindled all swore on oath that Beck was the man.

While Beck was in prison this particular type of crime disappeared but the moment that he was released the police started to receive complaints from other women. Beck was re-arrested and this time faced a much longer sentence. However, before he could be tried another man called Smith was caught, as it were, in the act and he confessed to having been responsible for all the crimes. Incidentally Smith would later be hanged for drowning some of his victims in a bath after marrying them.

Now the women who identified Beck were not merely being vindictive, they genuinely believed that Beck was the man and yet they must have individually spent some considerable time in Smith's company. Even more mystifying, Beck and Smith did not even look like each other. Again a whole number of eye-witnesses had inexplicably made an error.

Following the Beck case a committee under the Lord Chancellor issued rules for guidance in cases where identification was crucial to conviction. They advised that where identification could not be supported by any other evidence then it would be unwise to convict. But of course this was only a suggestion.

Psychologists have long been interested in this phenomenon and they have arranged a number of experiments but without any conclusive evidence as to the cause. One factor, however, would appear to be that given a witness with a healthy respect for authority then a skilled interrogator can easily persuade such a witness to agree to almost anything. I suspect that this had something to do with the evidence sworn to by the McHaffies.

Detective John Trench now gave evidence and his testimony gave the court and the public a glimpse of aspects not hitherto revealed. Trench had been present when Slater's luggage had been examined and he mentioned, almost as an aside, that Slater had an extensive wardrobe. This clearly surprised the judge:—

By the Lord Advocate:—How many boxes of clothes or bags did this man have?—There were seven bags altogether.

By the Court:—Were they all full?—They were all full.

By the Lord Advocate:—He had a great many suits of clothes?—He had a lot of clothing—good clothing.

By the Court:—And amongst them were old clothes; they were not all new clothes?—No, they were not all new, a lot of them had been worn.

And yet the Judge should not really have been surprised—or envious—by the fact that a pimp had a better wardrobe than he himself possessed. Pimps tended to be higher paid. What the judge should have remembered is that virtue itself is sufficient reward.

The point the defence was interested in was the mechanism of the identification parade:—

By McClure:—The prisoner was placed in a row with eleven other men; was there any foreign-looking men amongst them?—No; they were all Scotsmen, I think.

No person of dark complexion?—There were some of dark complexion.

And of foreign appearance?—No; not of foreign appearance.

So that anybody looking for a foreigner, of course, would go straight to the prisoner?—Possibly, yes.

That is an irregular way of conducting an identification, is it not?—I do not think so.

I understood that when you were going to identify a person in connection with any alleged crime you

attempted to get him placed among men who were more or less like him; is that not so?—No; it is not.
Is that not the practice in Glasgow?—No; it is not.
Just as a matter of ordinary fairness, do you not think that it would be proper practice to observe?—It might be the fairest way, but it is not the practice in Glasgow.
Slater's photograph, as an obvious foreigner, had been published in the Glasgow papers before that?—Yes.
So that any person who had seen the photograph would look for a foreigner, and could not escape singling out Slater?—I do not think that they could very well . . .
Had you anything to do with the description which was published in the papers after this crime had been committed?—No, I had nothing to do with that.
Do you describe Slater's nose as a twisted nose?—No, I would not describe it as a twisted nose.
Was that not the way it was described by the girl Barrowman?—I could not say; there were so many rumours and stories that I did not pay any attention to them.
Has the Glasgow public not gone pretty nearly mad over this case?—I would not like to say that they have gone mad; it certainly has caused a lot of sensation and talk.
Have you heard that Miss Gilchrist was a resetter?—I have heard that frequently.
And that she kept uncut diamonds in her house, which she got from thieves?—Yes, I have heard that too.
Not a word of truth in it?—Not a word of truth in it, as far as I know.
Have you heard within the last fortnight a rumour to the effect that people have been back at her house tearing up the floors and throwing uncut diamonds, which were found under the floors, into the street?—No, I have never heard that story.
Have you heard that she was the mother of the servant girl, Lambie?—No.
But of another?—Yes.
Have you heard that she was the mother of Slater?—No.

May I take it that this case has given rise to extreme excitement among the Glasgow public, and to no end of unfounded rumour?—There is no doubt about that—all sorts of rumours.

Interestingly enough the rumours concerning Miss Gilchrist's sex life could have been quite easily scotched. The men who performed the autopsy could have said whether she had ever given birth or not.

There now followed a number of witnesses including one other policeman who all swore to having seen Slater near or about the close leading to Miss Gilchrist's flat in the weeks prior to the murder. If all these witnesses were telling the truth then Slater must have been haunting the area near to the flat night and day for he is placed there by more than a dozen witnesses at times varying between early morning and late at night. But each of these witnesses also claim to have been regularly in the street over the period and yet they each only see him two or three times.

There were two witnesses that first day, however, who cannot be so easily dismissed. A cabinetmaker, Robert Bryson, claimed to have been in West Princes Street on the Sunday night before the murder and that he had seen a man hanging about near to the close. "He was staring at the windows, and I thought that he was looking for someone or waiting for somebody." Bryson describes the man as wearing a dark coat and trousers and a black boat hat. He had a slight moustache with a slight droop. He walked rather slowly and sluggishly. The time was about quarter to eight in the evening.

The other witness was Andrew Nairn who lived round the corner in Queen's Crescent. He had been out with his wife and family visiting and they were retuning home along West Princes Street at about nine-fifteen. Nairn had got some distance ahead of his wife and while waiting for her to catch him up he noticed a man standing on the opposite corner. The man was broad shouldered and dark haired. He was wearing a light coloured coat and had on his head a motoring cap (a deer stalker).

In spite of their conflicting descriptions both men had easily identified Oscar Slater as being the man.

The final witness of the day was Helen Lambie. Slowly and surely she was taken through the events of the night of December 21. Helen had one new piece of testimony to offer. She was now claiming that on the Sunday night before the murder she had been out and when walking along West Princes Street at about 6.45pm she had noticed a stranger. "I saw a man passing back and forward on the same side of the street as I was on. He was wearing a dark overcoat and a bowler hat. I could not say whether he was clean shaven or not but he had a sallow complexion."

By McClure:—You say that you could not recognise the man that you saw on the street that Sunday?—Yes.

And so little did you think of it that you did not mention it to anyone at all until March 12?—Yes.

You had been in America in between, and you had been examined by the fiscal at different times, but you never thought of the man walking on the street on December 20 until March 12?—No.

You said that you could not recognise him?—Not the one that I saw on the Sunday night.

I wish to ask you this—what did you recognise in the man in the hall which enabled you to identify him afterwards in America?—By his walk and height, his dark hair, and the side of his face.

Is it not a fact that you were not quite sure of him to begin with when you saw him in America?—Yes, I was quite sure.

I wish you to be careful about this. In America, when you were asked if you saw the man present you said at first, "one is very suspicious, if anything"?—That is a mistake.

These were your words?—Yes, I quite believe it.

When the question was put to you you said, "one is very suspicious if anything"?—Yes, because he walked up and down.

That was after you had seen the man walking. You were asked, "Now, do you see the man here you saw that night?" You said, "one is very suspicious if anything."?—It was the way that it was put. It was what Miller meant.

But you used these words in America. What did you mean by that?—Because it was the same man.

Why did you say that you were suspicious?—It was a mistake.

You mean that you did not say what you intended to say?—Yes, I did not intend to say that.

You have told us today that you recognised him by his face?—The side of his face.

I will read the question again that was put in America. "Now, will you describe, please, this man that you saw on that night who passed you at the doorway, the height if you can tell, the clothes if you can tell or any other description of him that would in anyway identify him to anybody else?" And your answer is, "The clothes that he had on that night he has not got on today, but his face I could not tell." Did you say that?—Not the broad face but the side.

The Commissioner said, "What did you say about his face?" and your answer is, "I could not tell his face; I never saw his face."

Now, when you said these things in America and stated on two different occasions that you never saw the face, why do you go back on that now and say that you saw the man's face and recognise him?—I did see his face.

Why did you say then that you had not seen it?—There has been a bit left out.

Did you say in America that you did see his face?—I do not remember.

Why do you say that a bit has been left out?—Because if I did not say it there then I could not say it here.

You are now speaking at a distance of many months, four months and more, since you saw the man in the lobby when your recollection was fresh, on January 26, just a month after the occurance, and you said that you had never seen his face at all. How do you explain that?—Because he did not look at me, but I saw his face when he was going down stairs.

Why did you not say so before?—I am saying it now.
Why then did you not say it in America?—(no answer).
Here is another question I wish to ask you about. What did you mean in America by saying that you could not tell the man's face, that you never saw his face, if, in point of fact, you did see it. What did you mean by that?—Nothing.
Why do you contradict it four months afterwards?—It is not four months since I said that. It is less than that.
It is three months then, is it?—Yes.

Try as he may McClure was never going to get a satisfactory answer to his questions and he must have been aware that by continuing without the assistance of the court he was coming dangerously close to defeating his own purpose. For the ordinary citizen sitting in the jury box the struggle must have seemed one-sided, the skilled advocate against an uneducated young maid. Without the intervention of the judge, and the judge during the course of the trial never hesitated to intervene during the examination of other witnesses, then the jury could be pardoned for believing that Helen was more confused than deliberately prevaricating. But in spite of appearances Helen was not confused. She had been under pressure for more than an hour and yet her mind was quick enough to pick up McClure's mistake about the length of time.

In the dying minutes of the day McClure turned to the question of just how widespread the knowledge of Miss Gilchrist's jewellery collection was:
McClure:—Did anyone in the neighbourhood know that she was a person who kept jewellery in the house?—Some may.
But do you know of any?—Yes.
Who?—A girl friend of mine whom I told that Miss Gilchrist had a lot of jewellery.
But except for that girl you have no notion of anyone else who knew?—No.

Did you inform a man named Nugent that she had jewellery?—Yes.
How long ago was that?—Shortly after the New Year. (1908).
Last New Year?—The year before.
Did Miss Gilchrist used to have a dog?—Yes; an Irish terrier.
What happened to it?—It got poisoned.
When was it poisoned?—I think on September 7th or 8th last.
Was that thought to have been done by somebody?—I did not think it because I though it might have eaten something; but Miss Gilchrist thought that it was poisoned by somebody.
Intentionally to kill the watch-dog, was that the idea?—She did not say.
What did she say?—She thought that it was a shame of anybody to do such a thing to a dog.

When McClure finally sat down the Lord Advocate exercised his right to repair any damage that might have been done to his case:—

Lord Advocate:—Did Nugent visit you at Miss Gilchrist's house?—Yes.
Did he, on one occasion at least, have a meal in the house?—Yes; dinner.
And did Miss Gilchrist know that he came into the house, and was she quite pleased that he should?—Yes.
Is Nugent the least like the prisoner?—Not the least like.

The question as to whether Nugent was similar in appearance to the prisoner was quite improper for that was a matter of opinion. Had the Lord Advocate been really serious then his correct course should have been to bring Nugent into the court, stand him alongside the accused and let the jury make up their own minds.

CHAPTER 17

When the court reconvened the next morning Inspector Pyper was the first witness. Very rapidly he was taken through his version and the friction between the two divisions raised its head when he was asked whether he had any prior knowledge of the raid on Slater's flat. "No, I did not," was the reply. When it came to his turn McClure questioned Pyper first about the extradition trial but Pyper stonewalled and backed the previous witness. McClure then turned to Slater's luggage.

McClure:—In America you took possession of Slater's luggage?—Yes.

Have you been through the whole of his luggage?—Along with Mr Warnock I went through it all.

You went through it with the express purpose of finding garments in his baggage which would tally with the descriptions you had got?—Yes.

And also with the purpose of, I suppose, looking for blood stains?—Yes.

May I take it that there is no coat, waistcoat, or pair of trousers found in his baggage which bears the slightest appearance of blood?—I saw no blood on any of his garments.

And you searched for it?—Yes.

Did you find a pair of brown boots?—No, I did not.

Did you find other boots?—Yes, I think there was another pair of boots and some slippers.

Do you mean that there was only one other pair of boots?—Yes, there may have been more but I do not remember.

But were you not searching?—I looked simply for garments that he was described as having been seen wearing, or I was looking for blood stains.

Did you find what is commonly called a Donegal hat anywhere?—The hats that have been produced are the only hats that I found.

There were more than those hats that have been produced?—I do not remember seeing any more hats.

I put it to you that there were about seven or eight hats and caps in his baggage?—That is possible. I did not see them.
There is none that you would describe as a Donegal, and you did not find brown boots. Did you find any checked trousers?—No, I do not think so.
Any fawn spats?—No, no spats at all.
A great many coats?—Yes.
And they were all minutely examined?—Yes.
From the condition in which you found the room, and from the amount of blood that was spread about, can you conceive of the man having executed the murder without having splashed himself a good deal with blood?—I would fancy that he would have blood on his clothing.
A lot of blood?—Yes, I would say a great deal . . .
Now, about this hammer. Take it that the head of the woman was extensively smashed so that the brains were out in portions and that the head had deep holes in it, is that weapon that you have in your hand the least likely to have caused the injuries to that extent?—It certainly would have required a great deal of force to do it.
Is it in the least likely to be the weapon to do it?—I would not say that it is not.
But would you say that it was?—I would not like to say.
Would you not have thought that a hammer with a larger surface would have been necessary for the extensive smashing?—I would not say so.
That is a light hammer?—Yes, but if it was used with force it would have bad effects.
Show me where the blood stains are on the hammer?—I do not say that there are any.
Is it your theory that the hammer has been scraped?—It seems to me to have been scraped.
Is it your theory that the handle has been varnished originally or anything of that kind?—You can see that it has been tampered with in some way. Something has been done in the way of cleaning it up.

Do you see coal dust at the top of the stick where it joins the hammer head?—Yes.
Towards the lower part of the shaft, where there is a difference between it and the upper part of the shaft, does that not look as if a dirty hand has grasped the hammer?—It is possible.
Look at the new hammer which we have produced. Is that an exact replica?—Yes.
The same size exactly?—Yes.
Has it not got the same kind of handle?—Yes.
Is there any more sign of scraping on the one than the other?—The one is new and the other has been used.
But is there any sign on either of scraping up towards the hammer head?—Yes, the new hammer is all the same, whereas the other is smooth at the top and the bottom half is rough.
Suppose that somebody with a hand covered with coal dust gripped this new hammer, would you expect that the clean hammer would become exactly like that after a little use?—It might.

McClure was wasting his time if he expected Pyper to admit any more than the faint possibility that the hammer produced in court was anything other than the murder weapon. After having gone to the trouble of buying a replica hammer the defence should have got hold of the head of a newly killed sheep and tried to reproduce the wounds. It is almost that certain that the hammer would have broke before the skull.

Arthur Adams now had his turn to tell his story and he did so with a sense gravity and seriousness not obvious in many of the other witnesses. In sombre tones he described standing on the landing ringing Mrs Gilchrist's door-bell, of the man appearing from the spare bedroom and of the discovery of the old woman's body lying battered on the floor.
McClure:—Were you present when the girl Barrowman and the girl Lambie made their statements in America?—Yes.
And they both made their statement before you did?—Yes.

And, of course, they had both indicated that Slater was very like the man before you gave your evidence?—Yes.
And even after all you heard you do not give an absolute confident opinion that that was the man?—No, it is too serious a charge for me to say from a passing glance.
Do you say that all you had was a passing glance?—Well, you know the time that it takes for a man to come from a room.
You identified him as a clean shaven man?—I meant from here (indicating the upper lip); but there was little of it.
Did you not say clean shaven?—If he had a moustache he had not got anymore than I have got, and that is not much.
You are not clean shaven?—Well, very near it.
I see that in America you were asked, "What did his face look like?" and you said, "Just an ordinary face, a sharp featured man, nothing special about him, clean shaven."?—Yes.
And that is what you mean still?—Yes.

Thus in spite of having seen Slater a number of times in the flesh over a period of three months Arthur Adams was still not prepared to swear definitely that Slater was the man in the hall. McClure now turned to the question as to exactly where Helen had been when the man had appeared.
McClure:—The door was opened by Lambie who had the keys?—Yes.
Now, did you stand on the mat outside?—No, I stood over the threshold of the door.
Where did Lambie go?—Lambie made straight for the kitchen.
Now, when the door was opened for the first time was there anybody in the hall?—No.
I think that I heard you say that Lambie had got along as far as the clock on her way to the kitchen before the man appeared?—That is so.
Then it would be incorrect for Lambie to say that she

was at the door when the man passed her?—Well, I think so, but I think that the girl was excited.
That is not in accordance with her recollection?—I have nothing to do with her recollection.
At the time when the man passed you where was Lambie?—She was in the hall.
By the clock, you mean?—No. The man passed, and she went into the kitchen and just came out and told me it was alright. I took that to mean the pulley in the kitchen.
Where was the man who had come out of the room when Lambie came back and said to you, "It's alright."?—He was down the stair.
As I understand it, as you stood in the door the man was walking towards the door from the right hand side of the hall?—Yes.
And Lambie was going towards the left-hand corner to get into the kitchen?—Yes.
How far had the man got down the stairs before you started going down after him?—I had just time to go into the room. I looked into the room and the girl said, "Oh, you go down the stairs as quick as you can," and I went down stairs.
Can you give any idea as to how long you would be in the house after the man had passed you at the door before you started after him?—Not more than half a minute.

Arthur Adams was clearly wrong in his estimate of the time lapse between the stranger exiting hurriedly and his taking up the pursuit. Helen went first into the kitchen where she had to turn up the gas. She then went into the bedroom where she looked around.

Finally she went into the sitting room, came out, and then went back in with Arthur where they both stood and stared at the body. Far from half a minute elapsing it must have been a good two minutes or more before Arthur set off in pursuit.

Of the evidence of Mary Barrowman I will say nothing. No one who reads the record of the trial can read her evidence with any feeling of belief.

As we already know only too well West Princes Street at night time was a very quiet street indeed. There must be a strong probability, then, that if Rowena Adams really did see a man loitering outside the close leading to Miss Gilchrist's flat at 6.55pm then that man was almost certainly the same man seen coming out of the bedroom a quarter of an hour later. Rowena describes the man. "He had a long nose, with a most peculiar dip from here (pointing to the bridge of the nose) You would not see that dip among thousands. He had a clean complexion but something of an ivory colour. He was very dark, clean shaven and very broad in this part of the head (points to temple). He had a low-down collar. His cap was an ordinary cap, I think of brownish tweed. He was very respectable looking.

McClure:—You have forgotten to mention to us that the man was wearing a coat?—He had on a heavy coat.

A tweed coat?—I believe it to have been brownish tweed.

A heavy coat?—I believe so.

Not like the waterproof that has been produced?—Let me see the collar.

Have you not seen this before?—No; they have not bothered me before but just once. Show me the hem.

Did you see the hem that night?—Yes. I am going by the hem considerably, because it was not a thin paper-like edge. It was a hemmed edge, whatever the coat was.

Do you mean a heavy seam inside the edge of it?—It was not like a thin waterproof.

It was not like the waterproof which has been produced?—It was not that material. I have stuck to that all along and I will stick to that still.

You have also said that it was not a fawn coat?—Well, first of all, I said it was browny fawn, but Mr Hart (fiscal) seemed to have a good deal of difficulty about browny fawn, and so I was quite agreeable that it should pass as a coat the predominant colour of which was brown.

You were ready to slighty change the colour to please

Mr Hart?—No. I have said all along that it was brown or fawn. Of course, there are so many shades you see.
I understand. It was a brown coat and a heavy coat. When did you first make a statement about this man?—On the Wednesday following the murder.
Your brother was the first man on the spot?—Yes.
Did you mention this man to him?—I mentioned it on the Wednesday and they laughed at the matter.
Why?—They said, "What was the man doing. What had he to do with the murder?" That was very reasonable.
May I take it that your family treated the alleged man rather as a jest?—They did and they said, "There are quite enough mixed up in this miserable affair."
The man you saw you thought was rather delicate?—He was not standing as a robust man would.
Were you surprised when you saw a man of Slater's build at the police office?—Very much so.
He was not like the man you had seen?—The face was there, but in that coat he was totally different from what he was in the first coat.
The delicacy you spoke of was absent?—No. He did not look the same figure in the waterproof. He did not look so nice as in the blue coat. He was a fine figure in the blue coat.
The waterproof did not show him off so well?—No.
Neither the waterproof nor the blue coat is the coat that you saw him in that night?—No.

Rowena Adams or Liddell unfortunately came over as being a foolish woman with all her talk about coats of various colours. At one time she even left the witness-box and crossed the well of the court to the dock in order to see Slater all the closer, getting him to turn the one way and then the other. In the midst of this nonsense what was missed was that she was giving a description, and a remarkably accurate one at that, of someone who most certainly was not Slater. Her man had a quite unique nose and in Glasgow's damp rather that cold weather he sported a heavy tweed coat rather than the lighter rain coat. People who stayed out in the country tended to wear heavier clothes than were generally worn in the city.

Professor Glasiter now gave his evidence and apart from his original reports all that he had to say that was new concerned stains on a waterproof belonging to Slater and the hammer which was being alleged to be the murder weapon.

McClure:—I understand that you cannot say that the hammer was used?—I cannot say positively that the hammer was used.

There is no trace of blood on it whatever?—We found certain corpuscular bodies that looked like blood, but I am not able to say positively that they were blood.

You cannot say that there was any blood on the hammer?—I cannot say positively.

You cannot say positively that the hammer was washed?—No. I said it bore the appearance of having been probably washed and scrubbed or sandpapered, but I cannot say it positively.

Do you observe that it has coal dust at the top where the handle meets the head?—I am not so clear as you are about that. I think that it is ordinary dirt, a collection of material which accumulates on any instrument that is exposed to the air in a dirty room.

If any washing of the hammer had taken place would that dirt have been washed up into the head?—It depends how it was washed. If it was washed by a scrubbing brush that is where they would try to get the dirt out.

We are now in the region of hypothesis?—Speculation.

So much for the hammer. I understand that you cannot say there is any blood on the coat?—For the reasons I have given you, that the corpuscular bodies, which I personally believe to be blood corpuscles, I cannot in a case like this be positive, because I cannot get the necessary corroboration from what was at my disposal.

And yet you would say it is blood?—Not in the absence of corroborative tests in a case of this kind.

Do you say that coat bears any trace whatever having been washed?—I said an application of water. I cannot say here that the appearance of the stains was due to their being washed, but I am clear that it was due to the influence of water.
Rain?—It might be rain.
That is what a waterproof is generally made to do, to keep rain off the body?—I think that I am aware of that.
Suppose that the murderer had knelt on the body of his victim and used an instrument like a hammer or a crowbar, looking to the extensive spattering of blood that there was about the room, would you not expect that the murderer would also be badly bespattered with blood?—I would expect the man who had applied the violence to have his clothes more or less bespattered.
To a large extent?—That, of course, would depend. Judging from the amount of injury in this case, I would say to very large extent.
His hands would not escape, I suppose?—I should think not, nor the hammer, or any instrument he employed.
He would be likely to have blood on his sleeves and hands?—He might have had gloves on—I cannot say.
Or on his gloves?—Anything that came into contact with the body would have blood on it.
Did you examine the coat that was found, internally as well as externally?—Yes, we examined certain stains from the interior of the coat.
And if a person put a bloody hammer into his pocket then the pocket would be stained with blood?—Yes, unless the hammer was wiped or washed beforehand.
Were there any stains in the pocket?—No.
So what you have given us today is the result of a thorough and exhaustive examination of all the clothing?—Yes, I think that I may claim that for the examination.
The result of your examination comes to this, that no blood has been found anywhere except on the rug,

upon the old lady's body itself and upon the various surroundings?—Your view is quite right, subject to the explanation I have already given with regard to the corpuscular bodies.
And you cannot say that it is blood?—I am not able to say here that it is blood, but I have no doubt in my mind.
Is that not a funny thing to say, a thing you will not swear to?—(no answer).
Is there anything except those articles in the room which I have mentioned which you can say are blood stained?—No. Putting it as you want me to put it, I cannot positively prove that anything found in the possession of the accused contained blood.
Any article of clothing?—Or an article found in the possession of the accused.
Lord Guthrie:—Looking to the length of the hammer, if the hammer had been put into any pocket of that coat would it have disappeared or would a portion stick out?—My recollection is that a portion of the handle, if it had been put head downwards, would have stuck out of the pocket by perhaps four inches.

The role of the expert witness is a peculiar one for the witness is there simply because of his expertise and not because of any special knowledge about the case in question. Thus although Glaister was employed by the Crown it was not part of the contract that he should help to secure a conviction. His job was to explain to the court, as best he could, precisely how Miss Gilchrist met her death and to assist in any other technical matters arising from the death. There was no requirement upon him to insinuate blood stains where no such stains existed.

It is interesting to note some of the advances which have been made in the science of forensic medicine in the eighty years which have elapsed since the Slater trial. For instance in the case of Miss Gilchrist no tests were made to detect the possible presence of foreign substances such as opium derivatives and yet it was known that she had been receiving and taking medication for some time before her death. It was known that Miss Gilchrist had not put up any struggle and this could possibly have been explained if she had been drugged before hand. I am not saying that she was drugged, but it was a possibility.

When a person dies the blood drains automatically to the lowest parts of the body where it gathers under the skin in dark patches known as lividity. As the blood also tends to thicken rapidly after death then these patches tend to remain where they have formed. Thus if say a body immediately after death is lying on its back and sometime later is moved so that it is lying on its stomach then the trained pathologist instantly knows that the body has been moved.

It was assumed by Glaister that Miss Gilchrist had been killed on the spot where she was found lying and yet, as he himself pointed out, the attack had two distinct elements, separated by some interval of time. Thus during the time between the elements the body could have been moved, indeed it might well have been the case that it was the moving of the body which was responsible for the two elements of the attack. The possibility that the body had been moved was apparently never checked out by Glaister. All in all the professor's effort had been pretty sloppy.

Superintendent Ord gave evidence dealing with the broader aspects of the investigation and when his turn came McClure wasted no time in turning his attention towards the alleged flight from Glasgow by Slater.

McClure:—Why did you say that you discovered that upon the Friday night that there were two single tickets taken for London?—That was reported to me. I had officers making enquiries at all the railway stations, and it was reported to me that two tickets had been taken for London.

And you naturally thought Slater and his travelling companion had taken tickets for London, and then changed to Liverpool to put the police off the scent?—Yes, I believed that at the time.

Have you discovered since that the Caledonian

Railway time books for that night show that two single third-class tickets were also taken from Glasgow to Liverpool, and that Slater and his companion travelled in a through carriage to Liverpool?—I have not discovered anything of the kind, because I have never seen any railway books belonging to any of the railway officials, nor have I interviewed them.
Look at production No. 69. You see the 9.05 train from Central. Did Slater travel by the 9.05 train?—I cannot tell you definitely because I was not there. It was reported to me that he was supposed to be travelling.
Do you find that two single tickets for Liverpool were issued for that train?—I see London, Birmingham and London mentioned here.
Do you see that two tickets for Liverpool were for the 9.05 train?—Yes.
And that these were the only two tickets for Liverpool that night?—That is all that is here.
Do you know whether the man's luggage was labelled "Glasgow Central to Liverpool?—I cannot tell you anything about that.
Are you satisfied now that the man did not start with London tickets?—No, certainly not.
Have you heard of any other people who travelled that night to Liverpool?—No, but it would take a great deal more than an entry in a book to satisfy me that Slater did not travel with London tickets.
And you are not satisfied that Slater went by train to Liverpool?—I am satisfied of that.
But not with Liverpool tickets?—I cannot say that.
Have you examined the labels on his luggage?—No.
Liverpool, Lime Street, is on his luggage?—Yes.
Is it probable now that he travelled with London tickets?—Yes, very.
Why do you say so?—Because I know that he covered up his tracks as far as he could.
Have you got any information that Slater took out two London ticket at the station?—Yes.
From any person who still remains of that opinion?—Yes. There is an official of the Central Station I believe

who could have spoken to that if his name had been on the Crown list.
So that the only person who could have proved that Slater and this woman took tickets for London and then changed to Liverpool is not present?—So far as I know. Of course the whole of that is hearsay. I was not at the station.
But everything is reported to you?—Yes.
That naturally would have been a very suspicious circumstance if a person had taken a London ticket and changed to Liverpool?—Yes.
Do you still persist in saying that that is what Slater did?—I do not say that I persist, because I do not know definitely.

On January 4, through the good offices of Superintendent Duckworth of the Liverpool CID, Ord had in his possession a bundle of sworn statements which collectively accounted for Slater's movements from the moment he arrived at Lime Street until he sailed for America the following afternoon. The effect of all these statements were to show that whatever else his intentions might have been hiding his tracks from the police was no part of these intentions.

Even earlier than January 4, on December 28, Duckworth had been in touch with Ord by telephone to tell him the results of his investigation. This contact was maintained at intervals right up until the start of the trial. Duckworth also interviewed the ticket collector of the Glasgow section of the train from Wigan. He recalled taking the two tickets from Slater which he then, in accordance with the standard practice, handed in on the completion of the journey for return to the station of issue. Ord then could have checked the tickets surrendered by calling at Central Station, Glasgow. And I suspect that is exactly what he did. That is probably why the person who had issued the tickets was never called as a witness.

To deliberately conceal any evidence from the court is a criminal offence and that is what Ord quite deliberately set out to do. Better than anybody else there in the court Ord knew the truth about Slater's so called flight from justice. Clearly the wrong man was in the dock.

The remainder of the prosecution witnesses after Ord were of not any great importance so that with the Superintendent's evidence the prosecution was to all intents and purposes finished.

CHAPTER 18

Although under the presumption of innocence there is no need for the defence to lead any evidence in practice things do not work out that way. The fact is that juries like to see the defence put up something of a show and are inclined to regard it as a sign of guilt when the defence takes the attitude that it is entirely up to the prosecution to make out their case beyond a shadow of a doubt. But what could a man say who had first heard of the name of Miss Gilchrist when he had been wakened in the morning, 3,000 miles away from the scene of the crime, and told that he was being charged with her murder. It is the secret dread of everyone that such a thing should ever happen to ourselves.

The problem facing the defence was that in the only two areas in which they could offer any kind of real evidence the witnesses they would have to rely upon were unfortunately of a character that a jury would tend to disbelieve. To show that Slater had been preparing to leave Glasgow some days before the murder all that could be offered was the word of a dubious bookmaker's clerk and a couple of even more dubious dealers in dodgy jewellery. By way of an alibi for the time of the murder, that he was having his dinner at home at the time, Slater had to rely upon the word of a prostitute and her so-called maid. It was a question of credibility. It is not surprising then that the defence only took up a couple of hours of the court's time.

The Lord Advocate—according to William Roughead, a solicitor and well-known writer on Scottish crime and a contemporary of Ure—was notable for his unswerving belief in the guilt of anyone he ever prosecuted. In his final address to the jury in the Slater case he certainly lived up to his reputation. He had scarcely got into his stride before he was telling the jury what kind of monster they had before them:

" . . . he had followed a life which descends into the lowest depths of human degragation, for, by the universal judgement of mankind, the man who lives upon the proceeds of prostitution has sunk to the lowest depths, and all moral sense in him has been destroyed."

The motive, according to the Lord Advocate, and in spite of there being no mention of it in the indictment, "was as plain as daylight." It was robbery, and not for money, but for jewels. But how had Slater come to know that Miss Gilchrist was possessed of a valuable collection of jewellery? At this stage the Lord Advocate was unwilling to say but he did promise to do so later. Alas, like so many promises it was only made to be broken.

That Slater was a jewel thief of international standing the Lord Advocate had no doubts. "We hear a great deal in this case about his dealing with jewels from the selling point of view, but we hear nothing about his dealings from the purchasing point of view. No man was examined in the past three days who ever sold jewels to him. You may draw your own inferences."

In point of fact this was not quite true. In her evidence to the court Slater's mistress had claimed that the brightest jewel on Slater's stall, the infamous cresent brooch, belonged to her. But apart from that, which may or may not have been true, the brooch had received what amounted to world wide publicity and yet no one had come forward to claim it as their property. What is more with their belief that they were dealing with an international jewel thief then it is inconceivable that the Glasgow police had not enquired of other police forces as to whether Slater had a reputation as a thief. There is, in fact, not a scrap of evidence to show that Slater had ever stolen a thing in his life.

In spite of his earlier promise the Lord Advocate shied away from trying to explain to the jury how and when Slater came to know about the fortune in jewellery possessed by Miss Gilchrist. The nearest he came to it was in his veiled suggestion that Slater had quite deliberately chosen a flat to rent which was near to the scene of the crime. If this were to be carried to its logical conclusion then what he was suggesting was that the crime had been planned before Slater had even left London.

The Lord Advocate, however, really threw caution to the wind and embraced phantasy when he turned his attention to the witnesses who claimed to have seen Slater at all hours of the day and night in West Princes Street during the fortnight before the murder. Slater was there, because, "he required as part of his elaborate precautions to familiarise himself with the inmates of the house, with their movements and their habits, and also with the movements of the police. There was one method, and only one, by which that object could have been accomplished, and that was careful, prolonged and steady watching with a skilled eye."

If Slater had watched prolongedly with a steady and skilled eye why then had he chosen the moment to strike when he knew that he had only some five or so minutes by which to achieve his design? Any prolonged watch would have told him that Sunday morning, when Miss Gilchrist and her maid went to church, was the best time to break in. The house was empty every Sunday morning for two hours or more.

For a skilled international thief Slater had put on a remarkably amateurish show.

Ure was finally driven to make some comment on the evidence giving by one of the two chief witnesses, Helen Lambie. The Lord Advocate was not that stupid that he thought for a moment that Helen had been entirely credible. There was, he admitted, a discrepancy between her evidence and that given by Arthur Adams as to where Helen had actually been standing when the stranger had appeared. On the whole Ure tended to believe Arthur's version but he then went on: "When the man passed her she turned round and watched him until he had disappeared down the stairs. She therefore had an opportunity of seeing his profile, height, general appearance and walk". What the Lord Advocate failed to realise was that she could only have gained such a view had she been standing at the door. From inside the hall with the doorway blocked by Adams and the door she could not have seen the man walk down the stair.

The defence was only too well aware when McClure rose to address the jury that he was probably already pushing against a closed door. There was really very little that he could do except to appeal to the jury's sense of fair play:

"I must confess to a feeling of very great responsibility in rising to address you now on behalf of the accused. Not only has he got, with slight resources and the assistance of a few friends, to fight his case single-handed against the forces of the Crown and the power of the Lord Advocate, but I think that he has also to fight an unfair fight against public prejudice, aroused with a fury I do not remember to have seen in any other case. Certainly the newspaper campaign which has been conducted against this man Slater is without parallel for its absolutely irresponsible character, for the rumour it has set afloat, for the prejudice it has created. I am not saying this to you because I believe that you have been moved by it, but I mention it because it is right that it should be mentioned and condemned. This man, in many quarters, has been convicted before he has been tried; but I ask you to bear in mind that you, gentlemen, and all of us here who have been present during these last three days listening to the evidence, are better judges than any outsider can possible be of the rights and wrongs of this matter. If you had any preconceptions in your minds because of what you have seen in the newspapers before you were empanelled—even as late as last Saturday night there was a disgraceful attack upon the prisoner in an evening paper—lay that aside."

McClure then passed on to review the evidence against his client.

Lord Guthrie in his summing up did, and this is contrary to the opinion of many other writers on the trial, I believe, endeavour to be fair to the prisoner.

Certainly more fair than the Lord Advocate. He failed, however, on one point and later that point would be crucial. When discussing Slater's admittedly bad character he went on to say: "The Lord Advocate founds on the prisoner's abandoned character as a point in support of the Crown. He is entitled to do so, because a man of that kind has not the presumption of innocence in his favour which is a form in the case of every man."

There would seem to be grounds for some doubt as to whether Lord Guthrie actually meant the words to be taken so brutally for he immediately goes on to modify the force of his observation to some extent. But he did say the words and his modifications were not sufficiently strong to undo the damage. Lord Guthrie, if he is remembered for anything, is now remembered for that one sentence. He is known as the judge who tried to qualify the presumption of innocence.

After deliberating for just over an hour the jury returned with its verdict.

Clerk of the Court:—What is your verdict Gentlemen?

Foreman:—The jury, by a majority, find the prisoner guilty.

The Prisoner:—My Lord, may I say one word? Will you allow me to speak?

Lord Guthrie:—Sit down just now.

The Clerk:—Then this is your verdict, "The jury by a majority find the panel guilty of murder?"

The Foreman:—Yes.

Mr Morrison:—I move for sentence.

While the sentence and verdict were being recorded.

The Prisoner:—My Lord, My father and mother are two old people. I came on my own account to this country, I came to defend my right. I know nothing of this affair. You are convicting an innocent man.

Lord Guthrie (to Mr McClure):—I think think that you ought to advise the prisoner to reserve anything that he has got to say for the Crown Authorities. If he insists upon it, I will not prevent him—now, will you see what he says?

The Prisoner:—My Lord, what shall I say? I came over from America, knowing nothing of this affair, to Scotland to get a fair judgement. I know nothing about this affair, absolutely nothing. I never heard the name. I know nothing about it. I do not know how I could be connected with the affair. I came from America on my own account. I can say no more.

Lord Guthrie then donned the black cap and sentenced Oscar Slater to be hanged in Duke Street Prison, in Glasgow, on the morning of Thursday 27th May. Slater now had three weeks to live.

CHAPTER 19

Generally speaking the verdict and sentence was well received—better for Scotland that the perpetrator of such a brutal murder should turn out to be a German Jewish pimp than one of its own. But not all were of this opinion, a number were not at all happy at what had taken place at the trial. The morning after the sentence the Glasgow Herald voiced this feeling of disquiet.

From the court Slater was taken to a cell where he was held until the early hours of the morning. Although there were already plenty of motor cars about neither the roads nor the mechanical reliability of the cars was such that they could be trusted for use in the transference of the prisoner. After midnight Slater was taken to Haymarket Station where he boarded a private train which took him to the Springburn siding in Glasgow, a half mile from Duke Street prison. Once there he was dressed in the uniform of a condemed man. From this time on until the moment of his death he would never be alone.

Although in 1909 there were no Courts of Appeal the sentence passed by the court was not the last word. A Memorial could be presented on behalf of the prisoner to the Secretary of State for Scotland requesting the commutation of the sentence and on May 17 Slater's solicitors submitted such a Memorial supported by a petition which had been signed by more than 20,000 people.

The Memorial is a lengthy document but in essence it argued three points. Firstly, that the prosecution had made unjustified use of Slater's character although this had not been an issue at the trial. Slater had made no attempt to present himself as being whiter than white. Secondly, that the identification of Slater had been unsupported by any other evidence in direct contravention of the guide lines laid down after the Beck affair. Thirdly, that the evidence of one particular witness, Agnes Brown, whose written evidence had been used in

America at the extradition hearing had not been offered to the court.

This last point is worthy of some comment. Agnes Brown claimed that on the night of the murder she had been in West Princes Street on her way to night-school. She was a teacher seeking further qualifications. She claimed that at about 7.25pm she had been passed by two men running and one of them answered the description of Oscar Slater.

It would seem to me to be contradictory to argue against the unsupported evidence of eye-witnesses and then seek to introduce yet another eye-witness. More especially when the evidence she could give could only serve to destroy what little alibi Slater had. If Agnes Brown was right then Slater was not at home eating dinner but legging along the street in the company of another man. At the best it was only claiming that Slater should not be alone in the condemned cell.

Later others would seek to use the evidence of Agnes Brown and indeed to call her as a witness nineteen years into the future at a subsequent appeal. At the last minute, however, they would call off the attempt after being advised by the police. As at this time most of the policemen involved in the case were dead or at least retired then one can only wonder what was the dark secret in Agnes' past that made her a witness that no one would use?

As a purely normal procedure the Secretary of State sought the assistance of two colleagues in his review of the sentence of Oscar Slater. Before them they had the Memorial, the petition, and being polititions, probably the newspaper cuttings as well. They also had a letter from the presiding judge, Lord Guthrie. In his letter, again part of the normal procedure, Guthrie reviewed the evidence given at the trial and concluded that in his opinion the trial had been fair and that the verdict had been correct. However, in spite of his lack of doubt Guthrie urged the Secretary of State to commute the sentence to one of life imprisonment. This was rather strange given the brutality of the crime.

On May 25, less than 48 hours before the execution, the Governor of the prison entered the condemned cell to tell Slater that his sentence had been commuted to one of life imprisonment. The reprieve created little excitement. There were some grumbles about the general softness towards the criminal class and a couple of questions were asked in the House but the ripples quickly died away. After a few more weeks at Duke Street, Slater was transferred to Peterhead Prison in the north of Scotland where he would serve his sentence.

What many regarded as the final acts took place shortly afterwards. Almost every policeman who had played a role in the investigation were rewarded by promotions. The one exception was Detective Constable Trench. He had to wait three more years and then he was only promoted to Lieutenant. On the other hand Detective McGimpsey, who had hardly played a role at all except by accident, was promoted to Inspector. In the handouts the eye-witnesses were not forgotten either. A reward of £200 had been offered and with the end of the trial Mary Barrowman received £100 while Allan McLean received £40. The cynic might claim that the whole thing smacked of buying witnesses.

The show, everybody now thought, that had gripped the attention of Scotland and other parts far beyond her borders for so long was now over. They were wrong, they had only seen the finish of the first Act.

CHAPTER 20

In November 1913, Trench, now promoted to Lieutenant, was loaned out to the Broughty Ferry police to assist them in the solution of the murder of Miss Milne. The nett result of his intervention was that he turned a case which everybody thought had been solved into one which has not been solved even today. Such action hardly endeared him to his colleagues. There was also the little matter of his failure to defend the Glasgow police and their method of conducting identity parades. Trench might well now be the best known policeman in Scotland but among his colleagues he was not highly rated as a team player.

When he returned from Broughty Ferry, Trench was a man with something on his mind and he unburdened himself to a friend, David Cook, a Glasgow Solicitor. What Trench told Cook was that he believed that not only had Oscar Slater suffered a miscarriage of justice but that he had also been quite deliberately framed by the police. The problem facing Trench then was that because the officers involved were all high ranking officers it was impossible for him to do anything about it within the force. It was a classical catch 22 situation.

Cook had a friend who was the Inspector of Prisons in Scotland and so had the ear of the Secretary of State. Cook duely passed on the information to his friend and ultimately it arrived on the desk of the Secretary.

Trench was making three specific accusations. Firstly, that evidence had been available to the police even before the formal arrest of Slater when he came ashore at Renfrew that his so-called flight from justice had been nothing of the kind. Nevertheless the police had deliberately ignored the information and withheld it from the court.

Secondly, one of the witnesses, Mary Barrowman, had probably not even been in West Princes Street on the night of the murder. Had she been going, as she claimed, from her employer's shop to Cleveland Street then West Princes Street was well out of her way and would have added 15 minutes at least on to her journey. Even worse, there was good reason for believing that she had not gone to Cleveland Street at all on the night in question.

Trench had taken it upon himself to interview Mary's employer, Colin Maccallum, and had obtained from him a statement:—

".... I remember that some days after the murder of Miss Gilchrist, Barrowman's name was publicly, mentioned as an important witness. I saw from the daily paper that the girl was claiming to have seen a man leaving Miss Gilchrist's close. I also noticed from her statement that she was delivering a pair of boots at Howat's house on the night of the murder ... I was and am still convinced that she was not sent that message on the night of the murder, but several nights before ... Some time after Barrowman appeared in the case I drew the attention of Inspector Pyper to the fact. I showed him my books in support of what I said. Mr Pyper told me not to say anything about it, as it would upset the whole case, and he might get into trouble. He impressed upon me not to mention it to anyone, as the girl had insisted that she had gone the message on the night of the murder."

So not only had an important witness probably committed blatent perjury, but a senior officer of the police, and God knows who else, had conived at the perjury. Maccallum's sister corrobarated her brother's statement.

The third charge was the most serious of all and brings a new character to the stage, the mysterious AB:—

"I am aware that on December 22, the day after the murder, that Superintendent Douglas, along with Detectives Pyper and Dornan, drove in a taxi-cab to the house of AB. I am also aware that they did so in view of information supplied by Helen Lambie. I have endeavoured from time to time to elicit what took place in AB's house, but I am without information."

On the night of the murder Trench had been at Miss Gilchrist's flat but not being a member of the official investigation, being attached to the Central Division, he was not directly involved at this stage. He only got as far as the landing. The following day however, probably to his surprise, he was instructed by Superintendent Orr with the permission of his own Superintendent, Ord, to go alone to the house of Margaret Birrell and interview the lady with the purpose of finding out what she had been told by Helen Lambie when the maid had come to tell her about her aunt's death.

Now Superintendent Orr was the man in overall supervision of the investigation at that time and as such Douglas and Pyper reported directly to him. Immediately after the murder Pyper, and probably Douglas, had interviewed Margaret Birrell. On the morning after the murder Pyper had again interviewed Miss Birrell. In the normal course of events, then, Orr should have been privy to anything that the lady might have to say simply by reading the reports of his subordinates.

There is also some mystery attached to the fact that Trench was sent to conduct the interview alone. Miss Birrell was a potential witness and anything that she might have to say could possibly later form part of the evidence at a trial. But the law of Scotland demands that all statements must be corroborated by a second person at the time that it is taken or else it is useless as evidence and for that reason no policeman will ever conduct an interview without another policeman being present. Thus Trench must have been well aware at the time that he was not being used to collect official evidence.

Trench had been briefed to ask about one specific matter, what it was that Helen had said to Miss Birrell when she had come to her house to tell her about the death of her aunt? According to Miss Birrell Helen had said, "Oh, Miss Birrell, Miss Birrell, Miss Gilchrist has been murdered, she is lying dead in the dining-room, an oh, Miss Birrell, I saw the man who did it." To which Miss Birrell allegedly replied, "My God Nellie, this is awful. Who was it? Do you know him?" Helen then allegedly said, "I think that it was AB, I am sure that it was AB." A shocked Miss Birrell then responded. "My God, Nellie, don't say that . . . Unless you are very sure of it don't say that."

Miss Birrell then went on to tell Trench that on the night of the murder Pyper had interviewed her on that very matter and had told her that Helen had admitted to having recognised AB. On the Thursday morning, according to Miss Birrell, she had discussed the allegations with relatives and friends, including a member of the Glasgow Corporation who had then been in communication with Superintendent Orr.

On his return to the Central Police Station, Trench had made a verbal report to his superiors. Orr in particular had been very excited and according to Trench had exclaimed, "This is the first clue that we have." Ord was not so enthusiastic. Trench had then written up the interview in a report which had been given to Ord.

On Sunday, January 5, along with a detective called Keith, Trench claimed that he went to interview Helen Lambie at her aunt's house at Kinning Park. During this interview, according to Trench he had taken the opportunity to ask Helen about AB and in particular whether she was convinced that he had been the man in the hall. To this Helen allegedly replied, "Its gey funny if it wasn't him I saw . . ."

The next morning while making his report to Superintendent Ord, Trench claims that he mentioned what Helen had said to which Ord had replied, "Douglas has cleared all that up, what can we do?"

The police procedure with respect to the control of statements made in the course of an investigation was and is a well established one. All statements passed into the care of the office in charge of the investigation except in the case where a statement had to be handed over to the Procurator-fiscal. In this event a copy of the statement was recorded into a special book specifically held at the station for that purpose only. Thus on the completion of an investigation the police had for their files every statement taken or a copy of every statement. When Trench, during his unofficial investigation had turned to this file to his surprise he could not find any trace of his two reports. Even more mystifying he could find no statement which made any reference to AB. As far as the record was concerned AB had never existed.

In the light of the serious allegations made by Lieutenant Trench, McKinnon Wood, who was the Secretary of State at that time, had little choice but to order an inquiry. The man he chose for this was Sheriff Miller, Sheriff of Lanarkshire. Miller was given, ostensibly, wide powers but in fact his area for movement was strictly limited. In no way, he was instructed, was the inquiry to become a second trial. In effect this meant that no cross-examination of witnesses would take place nor, in spite of the serious allegations which had been made, could any witness be represented legally. Almost by definition the inquiry would also be required to be held in secret. In fact the procedure followed was that the witnesses were examined only in the presence of the Sheriff and his clerk.

The inquiry opened on April 23 in a room in the Sheriff's Court in Glasgow and after Trench had been heard the first witness to be called was Margaret Birrell. Miss Birrell dimly remembered being interviewed after the murder but she was not at all certain as to the precise date. She was, however, quite certain about one thing:—

"Helen Lambie did not say to me that she knew the man. She did not mention to me the name of AB when she came along to the house after the murder. At no time did she every say to me that she thought the man who left the house was AB . . . The statement, No2 of the inventory, has been read to me. It pupports to be a statement made by me to Detective Trench on December 23, 1908. I now solemnly declare that I never made such a statement and that all that is contained in it is absolutely false . . . I never heard of it being said that I had made such a statement until a few days ago, and it took me completely by surprise."

And what had the other party, Helen, to the conversation to say:—

". . . I remember on the Sunday night after the New Year of 1909 I had a visit from Detectives Trench and Keith. I do not remember them showing me a sketch of Oscar Slater on that occasion, and I was not asked to identify him. On that occasion neither Trench or Keith referred to AB. I did not say in answer to a question as to whether AB was the man I saw, 'its gey funny if it wasn't him' . . . The whole story is absolutely false. I did not know Oscar Slater before the night of the murder. I never saw him in the company of a man named Nugent . . . I wish to make it quite clear that neither to the fiscal nor to the police, nor to anyone else, did I make the statement that AB was the man I saw leaving the house."

When Trench allegedly interviewed Margaret Birrell her friend, Charles Cowan, had been present and he had been able to corroborate her version of the event. The alleged interview with Helen had been something else. On that occasion Trench had been accompanied by another detective so he was now the person who had the corroboration. Alas for poor Trench his erstwhile colleague was now a Detective Inspector and not at all willing to do anything which might affect his recent promotion:—

"On January 2, 1909, I went, along with Detective Trench, to 15 South Kinning Place, the house of Helen Lambie's aunt. I do not remember Trench taking a pencil sketch of Oscar Slater out to Helen Lambie. I have no clear recollection of what occured there. I have no recollection of Trench bringing the conversation round to the question if she knew the man who had left Miss Gilchrist's house, although it is likely that this was done. There was not such a word said in my presence as a suggestion from Trench that AB was the man that

Helen Lambie saw leaving the house. If such a thing had been said then I would have remembered it . . . My recollection is that we went to the house of Helen Lambie's aunt on our own initiative without being sent by anyone."

Junior detectives in the middle of a major investigation do not go swanning off as their fancy takes them in order to interview one of the principal witnesses. It follows then that Keith was probably lying when he claimed that they had set up the interview on their own initiative. It is also unbelievable when he claims that they did not take with them an artist impression of Oscar Slater. Slater at that moment was already in the custody of the New York police and the big drive in Glasgow could only have been to discover every possible fact about Slater's stay in the city. Every detective at that moment must have been carrying a copy of such a likeness.

Keith demonstrates a curiously selective memory in as much as the only part of the interview he clearly recollects is that part which fatally damages Trench's case. Selective memory at that time seems to have been endemic among the Glasgow police.

As it was part of Trench's case that the interview with Helen had been on the instructions of Superintendent Ord then what has Ord to say about it and the interview with Miss Birrell:—

"I did not give Trench any instructions to visit Helen Lambie at the house of her aunt and I did not give him any pencil sketch of Slater."

And what about the alleged interview of Miss Birrell? "I never heard Lieutenant Trench get any instructions to take a statement from Miss Birrell. I am certain that he did not return and inform Superintendent Orr and myself that Miss Birrell had said that Helen Lambie had told her that the man she saw leaving the house was AB. I am astonished to hear such a statement made, and I say quite solemnly that it is not true."

But Margaret Birrell admits that the interview did take place, her only doubt being as to whether it took place on the day claimed. Given that she was speaking about an incident which was five years old then her doubt is hardly surprising. So what is Superintendent Ord saying when he claims that neither he nor Orr authorised the interview nor were they aware of it at the time? Is he seriously suggesting that an ordinary detective could go into another police division and conduct an independent inquiry into a major investigation and they never knew anything about it? It is unbelievable. More especially when it is extremely doubtful as to whether Trench even knew of the existence of Miss Birrell on the morning after the murder.

By 1914 John Orr had been promoted to the rank of Assistant Chief Constable and in his evidence to the inquiry he backed up Ord. "I do not recollect giving instructions to Lieutenant Trench to visit and take statements from Miss Birrell . . . I do not recollect any information as to a statement by Helen Lambie implicating AB . . ."

Margaret Birrell had stated quite categorically that on the morning after the murder she had spoken to a member of the Glasgow Corporation who had, as a consequence of the conversation, communicated with Orr. The question then must surely be, if the conversation was not about AB then what was it about?

If Trench was in serious trouble over AB then he could expect no alleviation of his problems when the inquiry turned to his second charge, the evidence of Mary Barrowman. Colin Maccallum too had now changed his story:—

". . . On December 21, 1908, I am quite sure that Mary Barrowman did go with a pair of boots to Mr Howat. I cannot say whether there was an entry to that effect in my books because the books have gone missing. . . . I have no reason to believe that Mary Barrowman did not go on that message on that day . . . I did not make the statement to Lieutenant Trench that is contained in No 15 of the appendix. I did meet Lieutenant Trench on December or January last. I did not state to him that I was and still am convinced that Mary Barrowman was not sent the message on that night. I never said to Inspector Pyper that Barrowman had not gone that message nor did I show him my books. The statement is absolutely false."

As with his previous statement his sister once more dutifully endorsed her brother's words. There seems to be nothing that Miss Macallum would not do for her brother.

Remarkably enough there was and still is a precognition made by Maccallum in February, 1909, a few weeks after the murder. This statement, which was made before a sheriff and under oath, matches word for word the statement that Trench claims was made to him by Maccallum four years later. If this statement was then, as he was claiming, 'absolutely false' then he was confessing to having committed perjury in February, 1909.

The main thrust of Trench's allegation, that Maccallum had told him that Mary had not been sent that message that night, was substantially true. As the witness was, by his own admission, a self-confessed perjurer then we may only suppose that his tale about the book which could have shown whether Mary Barrowman did or did not make the delivery to Howat that night having gone missing was probably a lie as well. He more likely than not deliberately destroyed the books.

The only thing that Trench had seemingly got wrong was the bit about Pyper's reaction to his discovery that Mary had probably not been in West Princes Street on the night of the murder. But this could have been a bit of dressing up the incident by Maccallum. One thing is certain, the fact that he was precognoced is sufficient proof, that at the time of the murder the police had made no attempt to subborn Maccallum. The same, however, cannot be said for the days preceeding the inquiry. Quite clearly it was the police who had persuaded Maccallum to lie to the inquiry.

The third charge, Salter's alleged flight from justice,

was never considered although all the evidence collected by Superintendent Duckworth was handed over and Duckworth himself appeared before the inquiry. The reason given was that the evidence had been available to the defence at the time of the trial and if they did not choose to lead it then that was their misfortune. The inquiry, after all, was not a second trial.

With the evidence before the inquiry, and it must be said with the Sheriff showing no great zeal in the pursuit of truth, then the outcome was all too predictable. Trench had failed to make his case and therefore must pay the penalty. On September 14, 1914, at a meeting of the Magistrates Committee, John Trench was dismissed from the force. His crime? "That he communicated to a person who is not a member of the Glasgow Police Force, namely David Cook, Solicitor, information which he had acquired in the performance of his duties."

His ex-colleagues, however, were not finished with him yet. Trench had joined the army on his dismissal and in the early summer of 1915 he was arrested and charged with dishonestly handling stolen goods. David Cook was also charged along with him.

The charge arose out of a common but dangerous practice of all police forces. When goods were stolen a reward was often offered by the insurance company and if the reward was large enough it was not unknown for the thieves to sell the stolen property back. Inevitable in such negotiations the officer investigating the theft was involved for part of the deal usually included no arrests being made. Trench and Cook had been involved in one such case and this formed the basis of the charge. At the subsequent trial Trench was able to show that he had entered into the deal with the full knowledge and agreement of his superiors and both men were found, not guilty. The judge remarked that the prosecution was a disgrace.

Trench was, and still is, regarded as being an outstanding policeman of his time but in his handling of his allegations against his colleagues it must be said that he acted foolishly and against his best interests.

That what he alleged was true is no longer doubted and I suspect that at the time many people knew that this was the case. But did he really believe that the people against whom he was alleging corruption and the subordination of witnesses would throw away the habits of a life-time and tell the truth? Of course they wouldn't. With their backs against the wall they could only be expected to react in the only way they knew.

Nor should we have any reason to believe that the political authorities would welcome the prospect of the scandal becoming public knowledge that the biggest police force in Scotland was corrupt. If Trench won his day the Chief Constable, an Assistant Chief Constable and innumerable superintendents and inspectors would have to be jailed. The only way that state of affairs could be brought about would have been if there existed no other alternative. But there was an alternative, the accuser could be made the guilty man. One man against the upper echelon was no contest.

So why did Trench embark upon such a suicidal road? It is doubtful whether it was out of any desire to see Slater set free. During the whole inquiry Slater was hardly mentioned and he most certainly was not central to it. It is doubtful whether in Peterhead Prison he was even aware of the inquiry taking place. I suspect, and it can only be suspicion, that the real motive is to be found in the remarkable promotions that almost everyone who had been involved in the Gilchrist investigation received. I believe that Trench became so disgusted with a situation where detectives who could not even catch a cold, let alone criminals, were being promoted to Chief Inspectors, that he could no longer stomach it. His action was that of an angry and frustrate man who no longer cared.

After surviving the war Trench, like many others, fell victim to the flue epidemic that swept the world and he died in 1920. Rumour has it that he left behind his account of the arrest and trial of Oscar Slater but I very much doubt it. If he had then I would have imagined that it would have been published by now.

CHAPTER 21

The identity of AB is the enigma wrapped up in the mystery of the murder of Marion Gilchrist, or at least so it is always presented. Many a person has dined out well and often on the strength of supposedly knowing the secret. Over the years there have been many contenders for the position but, alas, when one digs a little deeper they are all found to be wanting. Now this is very strange for it is not as if the identity of AB was known only to a few, on the contrary his identity must have been known to a large number of people. To the top echelon of the police AB was a man of flesh and blood. To those involved in the inquiry, both in Edinburgh and Glasgow, all the clerks in the Scottish Office and the Justiciary though whose hands the papers inevitably passed, they would all know. Every person who was questioned about AB, Helen Lambie included, could easily recognise him in the street. No, AB was no secret, what he was was a red herring.

What do we know about AB? We know that he was some kind of relation of Margaret Birrell. According to John Trench's police diary produced at the inquiry, "Detective Cameron and I went along to Blythswood Drive on January 9, 1909, by instructions of Superintendent Ord. I went to No. 19 to warn Miss Birrell, and Cameron went to No. 23 to warn another family of the Birrells not to say anything about the story of AB, as it would do him no good and there was nothing in it."

Trench is supported in this by Cameron. "I, along with Lieutenant Trench, went to Blythswood Drive to call on Mr and Mrs Birrell. He went to No. 19 and I went to No. 23." There would seem to be some confusion in both Cameron's and Trench's statement. The records clearly show Margaret Birrell from time to time being listed as staying at No. 19 but there is no record of a Mr and Mrs Birrell staying at No. 23. If the couple then were staying at this address then it could only have been a temporary visit. There might, however, be a perfectly simple explanation for the confusion, the couple could have been staying with a married daughter. It is fairly clear however that AB was related to Margaret Birrell.

As is normal in murder cases all the close relatives of the victim are investigated and the many close relatives of Marion Gilchrist were no exception. But AB, it is fair to say, would seem to have been more closely investigated than the others, that at least is admitted by both Douglas and Pyper. So why then did they deny going by taxi to interview AB? The answer I believe is simple. The use of a taxi would suggest that AB lived out of town and some distance from a regular transport system. This fact could have identified him.

Was it Helen Lambie who, in spite of her protestations, directed the attention of the police towards AB? The answer to that question is that if it was not her then who else could it have been?

Helen knew AB which is hardly surprising as she had been a maid in the employment of Margaret Birrell before she went to work for Miss Gilchrist. In one of her many interviews Helen claimed that about a fortnight before the murder Margaret Birrell and a man, whom Helen is careful not to identify and whom her investigator is equally careful not to ask her about, visited Marion Gilchrist one afternoon. Like many maids, and who is to blame her given that male visitors were something of a rarity, it would seem that Helen was curious enough to listen. Not that she had much difficulty. Voices were raised and there was talk of money. Margaret Birrell did admit that shortly before the death of her aunt there existed strained relations between them over financial matters.

1908 had been a year of deep depression and many a businessman had gone to the wall because of it. All over Glasgow then at that time hard pressed businessmen must have been anxiously calling upon wealthier relatives for loans to keep them afloat until better times returned. Miss Gilchrist had her money safely invested and it would not be surprising then if one of her relatives should try to borrow from her and for there to be anger when the old lady rejected the plea for help. That, I suspect, was the reason for the rare visit and that was the reason, I also suspect, for AB to fall under suspicion.

Without any evidence it has always been assumed that if Helen did identify AB then she did so by suggesting that AB was the man in the hall. But that would have been far too specific and Helen did not like to be specific if she could avoid it. To direct the police towards AB all that Helen needed to do was to first tell them about the visit the fortnight previous and then to add that she had the fleeting impression that the man in the hall was AB.

One of the few things that we know is that when she was questioned on the night of the murder Helen resolutely refused to positively give any description of the man in hall. We also know, if Trench is to be believed, she was still not positively identifying AB two weeks later. The furthest she was prepared to go was to say that, "it was gey like him." We may also assume that whatever she did say about AB it was sufficiently vague for there to be no recriminations when AB was found to be clear.

The use of the first two letters of the alphabet as the non-de-plume to hide the identity of AB was no accident. The letter B quite clearly stood for Birrell and we may assume that the letter A represented the initial of the first name. As it turns out Margaret had a younger brother called Alexander. She also had another older brother called Samuel.

Margaret's father, also called Alexander, had been born in Old Kilpatrick, Dumbartonshire, in 1837 and he moved to Glasgow as a child. In 1852 he married Margaret Gilchrist, sister to Marion, and moved into what was to become the family home, a large flat at 6 Kelvinside Terrace. Alexander senior, was a parter in a firm called Walker, Birrell & Co. of Lyndoch Street. He died sometime around 1875 leaving a family of two sons and four daughters. His death at a relatively young age, he was only 38, could only have been financially disasterous for his family. Nevertheless they seem somehow to have managed.

Alexander junior, was apprenticed as a clerk to a firm in the finishing end of the textile trade and he seems to have been good enough at his job for by 1900 he was a partner in a similar textile firm, Crawford, Easton & Co. of Mitchell Street. This firm prospered for by 1908 it had moved to larger premises in John Street. Alexander also prospered for by the same year he was not only married, he had also bought himself a house in Ayrshire.

Samuel, the older brother, does not seem to have been any great success. He seems to have been married before the death of his father and I suspect that by 1908 he was living with one of his married daughters in Blythswood Terrace. Thus Alexander would appear to have been a major contributor to his family's financial well-being.

None of the girls of the family ever married, which would indicate a lack of a dowery. Margaret herself seemingly broke clear of the family home by establishing herself in a small massage business in Rupert Street which apparently was successful enough to enable her to maintain her own house in Blythswood Terrace. Her freedom also enabled her to have her friend, Charles Cowan, as a lodger. Margaret, incidentally, in the process managed to reduce her age by some seven or eight years which makes one wonder whether Charlie knew that?

By 1908 the British textile industry was already in a state of long-term decline and the depression of that year had hit the industry particularly hard. It would be surprising then, what with his new wife and new house, if Alexander found himself over-stretched and in need of a cash injection. That I suspect is what took him to his aunt's.

Helen disliked Margaret Birrell and the feeling was mutual. Miss Gilchrist was also aware of this dislike for on the last occasion that the aunt and niece met, two days before the murder, Miss Gilchrist deliberately went out of her way to praise the maid to Margaret. What I strongly suspect is that when Helen called upon Margaret to tell of her aunt's death she enjoyed the opportunity to settle old scores by hinting that the murder might have been committed by Margaret's brother. I would not put it any higher than this at the beginning but the reaction of complete terror manifested by Margaret at the possibility was sufficient to encourage Helen later that night to insinuate to Pyper that Alexander Birrell might well be the murderer.

While at this stage we may construct a reasonable case to show that AB was Alexander Birrell we have so far advanced nothing to explain how it was that all reference to AB was impunged from the record. Neither Alexander nor any of his close relatives would appear to have had sufficient clout, in spite of their modest success in life, to persuade the Glasgow Police to embark upon the wholesale falsification of the record. We must look elsewhere for that.

It was not uncommon, even as late as the early part of this century, for people to change the spelling of their names. My great grandfather, when he left Scotland for England, took it upon himself, for some unfathomable reason, to change the spelling of his name from Ramsay to Ramsey. For some equally unfathomable reason the Birrells also had change their name from its original Burrell.

Alexander senior, had been born Alexander Burrell and his parents were George and Janet Burrell. This couple had three boys, William, George and Alexander and when the family had moved to Glasgow from Old Kilpatrick, the father was in the shipping business on the canal, they set up home just off the New City road. Within a half mile radius of the parent's home all the family would eventually settle.

William, the eldest son, followed his father into the family business, and the business became ultimately known at William Burrel & Son. In time William married and in turn he fathered three sons, two of which, William and George would take over the family shipping business.

Sir William, as George's grandson would become, was something of a financial genius. His particular gimic was to sell all his ships at the time when the periodic trade cycle peaked. Thus obtaining the highest possible price for his ships. He then held on to his money until the inevitable slump forced down the cost of building new ships at which point he would go on a buying spree. In the course of doing this three or four times Sir William, and incidentally his brother George, became very rich men indeed.

Naturally this plunging in and out of the market tended to give Sir William a great deal of spare time which he spent in part in building up his art collection. He also spent a great deal of time in the discharge of his civic duties as a member of the Corporation. He became a councillor in 1899 and four years later he was elected on to the powerful Police Committee. The Police Committee ostensibly had no control over the day to day operation of the police and the members probably had no desire to interfere anyway. They were quite content with the control they had over appointments, promotion and discharges. Sir William served on this committee for more than three years, from 1903 to 1906, so that by 1908 most of the ranking policemen owed their good fortune, at least in part, to Sir William's grace and favour.

In spite of the change in the spelling of the name Sir William was the full cousin of Margaret and in 1908 they were staying within a quarter of a mile of each other. What would have been more proper than when the family were faced with a possible scandal that a cousin should come to the aid and comfort. This has always been one of the mystifying aspects about AB. None of the contenders advanced for the honour have ever had the necessary clout with the police. It never dawned upon any of the investigators that what they were looking for was not one person but two.

It is not too difficult to sketch in the broad outlines of the story surrounding the mystery of AB. When the attention of the police was directed towards Alexander Birrell by Helen he must have seemed a prime suspect. He was a man who had tried, unsuccessfully, only a few days before the murder to borrow money from the old lady.

The first reaction from the family, both Birrells and Burrells, was to find out precisely how strongly those investigating Alexander believed in the possibility of his guilt. To this end Sir William used his influence with the police committee to contact Superintendent Orr. But Orr himself knew nothing of the details without questioning his direct subordinates and this at that moment he deemed to be an unwise thing to do. Instead he sent Trench, a detective from another division, to try and find out precisely what Douglas and Pyper knew. He quite deliberately chose a moment when he knew that Douglas and Pyper would be out of town investigating the suspect.

In the event the investigation by Douglas and Pyper quickly proved that Alexander could not have possibly been involved in the murder and he was eliminated as a suspect. But to the family such an elimination, especially to the Burrell side of the family who were more prominant in the life of the City, it still left an unwelcome trace of scandal, people would say that there was no smoke without fire and tongues would certainly wag if it ever came out that Sir William had interfered himself directly. Thus it was not enough for Alexander to be cleared, matters had to be arranged so that he was completely expunged from the record.

Pressure again was exerted upon Orr and on the face of it the fears of the family could be easily met without any great trouble. By this time Oscar Slater was in the picture and no good purpose would be served by muddying the waters with an old suspect who had nothing to do with the murder anyway. So rationalised the police and they proceeded to remove any mention of Alexander from the record.

The expunging of the record in the event must have been a bit more difficult than had been first imagined. Statements in the form of filed copies could be easily removed and so their destruction was easy. The copies however which had been transferred into the Statement Book must have been less easy, it could not have just been a case of tearing out the offending statements a special way had to be found to accomplish the end.

Fortunately for Orr the current Statement Book was nearing its end and he used this fact very cleverly. Claiming that it was essential for all the statements concerning the Gilchrist murder to be kept in one book, he ordered that a new book should be opened and that the statement relating to the Gilchrist investigation should be transferred into the new book. During the transfer it was easy to lose any statement referring to Alexander Birrell.

Unfortunately for Superintendent Orr and his cronies the Statement Book was a legal document and as such to interfere with it in any way was a criminal offence. Thus when Trench raised the question of the missing files the threat was not directed towards the identity of AB, it was directed against his superiors. It was for this reason, and not for any feeling of tenderness towards AB, that Trench had to be destroyed. It was themselves who his erstwhile colleagues were protecting in the end.

CHAPTER 22

The war that was to end all wars finally past and the land that was to be fit for heroes to live in turned out for all too many to be a desert of unemployment and depravation. Meanwhile in his cell in Peterhead Prison Oscar Slater sat wondering if death was to be his only release. But if Oscar Slater was out of sight of the world the world at least had not forgotten him. Especially as money could be made from the memory.

The twenties was an era when crime, and more especially murder, became popular. Why this should have been so has never been satisfactorily explained although one popular explanation has it that it was a reaction to the millions of violent deaths that the world had been forced to witness. I suspect that the truth is that the phenomenon has a number of complex reasons. But whatever the cause the twenties was a time when the writings of Conan Doyle and Edgar Wallace reached out into millions of homes.

One of the more remarkable aspects of the phenomenon was the breadth of the market in sudden death. At one end of the scale the needs of the teenager and even of the pre-teenager was met by the adventures of Sexton Blake while at the other end the grandparents curled up at night with Sherlock Holmes. For the poor there was the lurid magazine, for the rich the well known series by William Hodge and Sons of Famous British Trials. Murder had become a very popular and profitable business.

The post-war years were also the time of great advance by the British press, that is in circulation rather than content. Against the tide of fictitious murder they offered the real thing. In news rooms all over the country a new breed of journalist was emerging, the crime correspondent. These were men who specialised in the reporting of crime and who, as the editor constantly assured their readers, had contacts throughout all the police forces from top to bottom.

The better known of these crime reporters enjoyed a public status about equivalent to that of a present day middle ranking pop singer. A journalist such as Percy Hoskins of the Express could add thousands to the circulation of their papers during a notable murder or trial. The trade, I suppose, reached its pinacle when crime reporters started to become the heroes of crime novels.

For the Sunday papers the approach to the profitable area of sudden death had to be somewhat different from the dailies. They tended to concentrate more in historical rather than the current murders. A Sunday newspaper would hire a famous writer of crime novels to write an article or even a series of articles about a well known but dated murder. Madeline Smith, in this respect, was a perennial favourite but Oscar Slater, simply because he was still in prison, had a fair run. Both Doyle and Wallace were to earn the odd pound or two writing about the Oscar Slater case. In this way the name of Oscar Slater was to be kept before the public.

In fairness to Conan Doyle, however, it has to be said that in his case his interest went somewhat further than merely using Slater as a convenient means of earning money. Doyle genuinely believed that Slater was the victim of a ghastly mistake and he devoted a great deal of his time and money in an attempt to rectify the mistake. In articles and letters to the press and Parliament Doyle kept up a constant pressure.

In July 1927, a Glasgow journalist, William Park, published a book called, The Truth about Oscar Slater, which was finally to have some effect upon the continued incarceration of Slater. Park had been a reporter in Glasgow in 1908 and he had covered both the murder and the trial. Consequently he knew and had spoken to all of the people involved in the case. He also knew a great deal about the background. He was, allegedly, a particularly friend of John Trench and it was claimed on his behalf, he unfortunately died before the book was ready for sale, that he had read the so-called journal written by Trench. I would doubt this solely on the grounds that I do not believe that such a journal ever existed but it is a fact that both Trench and Park shared a number of similar ideas.

Dr Adams had been the first medical man on the scene of the murder and it was normal practice for the first doctor to be called as a witness. In the case of Dr Adams this practice was not honoured and the good doctor felt slighted by the ommission. The truth of the matter was that Adams had been too free with his opinions when interviewed by Inspector Pyper and when the Procurator-fiscal learned of this it was he who had penciled out the doctor's name from the list of prospective witnesses. The case was going to be difficult enough without having a prosecution witness who would dispute the expert evidence of Professor Glaister.

The problem was that Adams had not confined himself to merely declaring Miss Gilchrist dead, the only role he was conceivably competent to perform. After examining the body the doctor had turned his attention to the possibility of something in the room having been used as the murder weapon. It has to be remembered that at this moment he was accompanied by Arthur Adams, the neighbour, who had doubtlessly told him that the man he had seen had not been carrying any obvious weapon. With the likeliest weapons, the fire-irons and other such portable heavy objects, yielding no satisfaction the doctor had turned his attention to the furniture. One of the chairs normally associated with the table was apparently some distance away from its usual position, it was near to the body, and one of the back legs seemed to be heavily stained with blood on all its four sides. The chairs were strongly built and heavy enough, in the opinion of Dr Adams, to have been used to inflict the wounds. This would account for the apparent lack of blood on the hands and clothing of the assailent for he would be protected by the seat of the chair from any splashing.

The chair would, however, in my opinion, seem to be

a scarcely credible weapon for a number of reasons. I must add that this view was also shared by both Pyper and Glaister. As can be seen from the photograph of the room the legs of the chairs were not joined together by stretchers which means that the individual leg would have to absorb the full impact of each blow. The bone making up the skull of Miss Gilchrist was unusually thick therefore it is doubtful whether the leg could have stood up to the punishment without breaking.

The major wound in the skull was roughly circular in shape while the back legs of the chair are clearly rectangular in shape. One would have expected then the edge of the major wound to have reflected this in some way. There was, apparently, also no attempt made by Dr Adams to examine the base of the leg which could be reasonably expected to have carried some sign of having been plunged deep into the skull.

Nor would the seat of the chair necessarily have afforded any protection from blood splashing. The bottom of the trouser legs and the shoes would still have been drenched in blood and yet no blood-stained foot-print was found.

Dr Adams died in 1922 but in the fourteen years that followed the murder he was interviewed by a number of people many of whom would later write about the murder. To all his visitors he maintained his opinion that the chair had been the murder weapon. Of course, following the trial, he had access to the report prepared by Glaister and therefore could now speak with the knowledge of the true extent of the injuries inflicted upon the victim. But this further knowledge, far from causing the doctor to modify his opinion, only served to confirm it more strongly. The hammer, he claimed, could not have produced the wounds to the head and in this he was right even if it was for the wrong reasons.

Most of us at sometime or another have been driving in a nail when we have missed the head and struck the thumb. The reason for this is that the head of the hummer is not moving in a straight line but along a curve. The blow then is not positive but glancing.

Now if the assailant had struck at Miss Gilchrist a sideways swipe, Miss Gilchrist standing and the head of the hammer moving in the horizontal plane, then either the outside edge of the eye or the nearside of the nose would have sustained damage. The likeliest result would have been for the nose to be sheared off. If the blow had been downwards, in the vertical plane, then the eyebrow or the top of the cheek bone would have sustained the damage. In neither case, or with the hammer head moving through any angle between the vertical and the horizontal, would the eyeball have been driven backwards into the socket.

If you slash the air with a light flexible cane then as everyone knows the cane bends. Now the fist gripping the cane is describing an arc but if the path of the tip were plotted then it would be found to be moving in nearly a straight line. As Newton so succinctly put it, any moving object will always try to move in a straight line unless a force is applied. For a hammer head to drive in an eyeball then it would help if the shaft were flexible.

Of course hammers are not made with flexible shafts but there is a well-known weapon that is quite deliberately made in such a manner and for the very reason I have given above. The cosh, black-jack, or sap, is a common enough weapon among the criminal classes. This weapon has a shaft or handle, about nine inches long, and made from rubber which has been moulded around a thin steel rod. The part that does the damage is roughly the shape and size of an egg with the shell made from rubber and the inside filled with lead shot. A short length of the thin steel rod is left exposed and to this the head is fixed and held by riviting the end of the rod. A weapon such as a cosh could very well in certain circumstances penetrate the eyesocket.

The line taken by Park in his book was that the murderer was possibly a relative of the victim although Park is careful not to claim this too boldly. As a journalist and a friend of Trench, Park probably knew the identity of AB. The motive, according to Park was that Miss Gilchrist had in her possession a document of some kind that the murderer wished to get his hands on. This does, of course, hint rather strongly that Miss Gilchrist was not averse to blackmail if not for money then most certainly for the power it gave her over her relative. Curiously enough having suggested the probability of blackmail Park then goes on to claim of the murderer, "He came without intention to murder, and he brought with him no weapon." This then surely begs the question, what means did he propose to employ in order to gain possession of the desired document?

The murderer waited nearby until he saw Helen Lambie leave the house. The moment that she had departed he approached the house and was admitted by Miss Gilchrist. Some kind of argument then ensued during which Miss Gilchrist received a blow which caused her to fall and to strike her head on the coal-box rendering her unconcious. Petrified at what he had done and knowing that he now faced a possible jail sentence he decided to complete the job. "He seized a chair and hacked away at the prostrate woman, in his haste to extinguish life and get away before Lambie reappeared on the scene."

The main weakness in this part of Park's theory, which also incorporates some of Adams ideas, is that there was simply not enough time. Helen left the house at seven o'clock, this much is at least established, and before five past seven the Adam's heard the noise of the attack. Indeed there was little enough time for the murderer to get from the street into the flat. Thus there was no time for any preliminary argument to take place prior to the attack itself. If Miss Gilchrist did somehow managed to admit her assailant, and this does not take into any consideration the fact that she lacked the means to open the door, then she must have been attacked almost immediately. In other words if this version is true, the murderer went to the flat with the express intention of killing the old woman.

Park in his description of the actual murder seems to have been in as much haste as his murderer for he fails to realise that he had now introduced a completely new element into the case. The coal-box was—and this can only be an assumption because no one actually ever stated the exact position of the coal-box and is based solely on a photograph of the room—situated immediately to the right of the fireplace and hard against the wall. But when the body of Miss Gilchrist was discovered, the head, which was nearest the fireplace, was eighteen inches from the fender and the coal-box did not protrude beyond the line of the fender. Thus for Park's theory to be right then the body must have been dragged a distance of two feet from where it originally lay to the spot where it was found.

Park was, of course, wrong, but not wholly wrong. The coal-box had fair signs of blood which Park argued was evidence of the head having struck the box. But if this was right then it would be reasonable to have expected a blood smear on the floor from the head as it was dragged to its final resting place? No such smear was found. Nor was the hair or clothing of the victim disarranged which is again what might have been expected had the body been dragged over the floor.

The motive suggested by Park also strains the credulity. If someone was willing to use violence in order to regain the alleged document then it is reasonable to suppose that the lady was well aware of its value. The flat had six rooms and a kitchen all filled with furniture in which to hide such a document. In the room in which the old lady was found dead there was a number of such hiding places to say nothing of a safe or strong-box concealed in the sideboard. Incidentally the existence of this safe was concealed from the court. Why then should Miss Gilchrist have hidden such a valuable document in a rather flimsy wooden box which might not even have been locked? And stranger still why should her murderer have, out of all the possible hiding places, guessed that the wooden box was the place to look.

The greatest strain in the credulity, however, is just what it was that the alleged document was supposed to contain?

An interesting footnote to the existence of the mysterious document is offered by Jack House, a well-known writer on the case. He suggests that the paper was in fact a copy of the recent will which cut off the sister of AB from her expectations. The murderer seemingly having been insisting upon her reinstatement when he lost the head and struck the old lady dead.

But while this might well account for the murder, although I must say that to me it would seem to be counter-productive to kill someone for such a reason, it in no way accounts for the search. What earthy good would it have done had the murderer found the document?

By a happy coincidence the publications of Park's book in July marked the start of the silly season for the newspapers and as a consequence the book received more attention than it might otherwise have reasonably expected. As interest in the case re-awoke reporters who had nothing better to do were switched to poke and scrape over its embers.

The Morning Post, at that time a leading newspaper of the right, commissioned Edgar Wallace, the famous writer of mystery novels, to review the book and the case. Wallace noted that at the trial, "No questions were asked of Lambie that were in anyway inconvenient to the prosecution." Perhaps it might have been more accurate to have said that no question were asked which might have been of inconvenience to Lambie.

The Daily News had a so-called correspondent who wrote under the by-line, The Pilgrim. This was a trick by which the readers were led to believe that the non-de-plume concealed the identity of someone in the know when in fact it was merely a device by which any reporter who happened to be available could be used. The Pilgrim had been used in similar stories with success and the good luck still held.

Mary Barrowman, described as being middle-aged although she could have only been around 33 years of age, was run to earth and persuaded to confess that for a fortnight before the trial she had been rehearsed every day by the Procurator-fiscal until her evidence was word perfect. She now admitted that her identification of Oscar Slater had been a lie and that the most that she had ever intended to say was that the Slater looked like the man.

The Empire News, a Sunday paper, hit the jack-pot when it allegedly ran Helen Lambie to earth in America and obtained from her a statement in which she *confessed* to having recognised the man in the hall. According to the article she now said that the man was a person who had visited Miss Gilchrist on a number of occasions and who had always been admitted by her mistress personally. For good measure she added that Miss Gilchrist had received a number of such male visitors.

This article created something of a sensation for it was assumed that Helen had identified AB. The close print, however, shows that nothing could have been further from the truth and that if Helen had given the interview then she was being just as vague as ever. But like so much else in this case while everyone was busy chasing hares the main point was completely missed. Helen had finally admitted that on the night of the murder she had told Pyper about AB. Trench had been right after all.

Early in 1927, before Park's book was published, Slater had managed to get a letter smuggled out of prison to Conan Doyle. In the letter Slater urged Doyle to make yet another attempt to get him set free. At no small expense to himself Doyle contacted every member of Parliament with a fresh resume of the case. On July 29, in the House of Lords the then Lord Advocate, William Watson, was asked whether there was any truth in a newspaper report that an inquiry into the case was being contemplated. Watson replied, "If there were then I would be very much surprised."

In fact the Government was becoming very much embarrassed by the whole affair and politically at that moment they were in a very weak position generally. The country had just come through the trauma of a general strike and while they had won the conflict the Government had received a severe shock. In the autumn of 1927 what the Government was desperately seeking was a period of tranquility.

During the summer recess Park's book was making its presence felt and the name of Oscar Slater was once more familiar to the populace in general. In the House of Commons, on November 10, Sir John Gilmour, the Secretary of State for Scotland, rose to answer yet another question about Slater. This time, instead of the standard answer, Sir John had something new to say. "Oscar Slater has now completed more than eighteen and a half years of his life sentence, and I have felt justified in deciding to authorise his release on licence as soon as suitable arrangements can be made."

It was to take a further long four days before the arrangements could be made and Slater could be set free. While I was writing this book I received a very interesting letter from a Mrs Close of Motherwell:—"I do not remember very much about the case itself but I was a maid in the Peterhead Governor's house at the time of Oscar's release. The Governor was ill in bed at that time so instead of being interviewed in the Governor's Office, Oscar was brought over to the house and I saw him there. The Governor gave Oscar a cigarette and I suggested that he keep the stub as a souvenir but it had been smoked down to the very last.

"As Oscar was leaving the house the Governor's wife was in the hall with her baby son in her arms. He showed a great interest in the baby and asked if it was a 'man child'. Oscar was a model prisoner and was known to be a very gentle man."

The following morning Slater was released to what may only be described as a hero's welcome. To the awaiting journalists he confessed to not having slept for the three previous nights. While welcoming the release the general attitude of the press was that the action had only been taken to head off a re-opening of the 1914 inquiry.

CHAPTER 23

The 1926 Criminal Justice Bill had included a clause which had set up a system of Appeal Courts but the Bill was not retrospective, it applied only to individuals who had been convicted after July, 1926. Nor was the new system to be treated as some kind of second trial, the convicted person could only base an appeal on grounds of sentence or on a point of law. Whatever else the primacy of the jury trial was to be maintained.

The release of Oscar Slater did not satisfy everybody, least of all the man himself. The nineteen years which he had served in prison was about par for the course in the case of a life sentence so that Slater had received little more than his due. Even worse the release in no way allowed for the possibility that he had been innocent. In law he was still guilty and could be re-called to prison at any moment without any reason needing to be given. The pressure was now on for this to be rectified.

But if Slater wished to clear his name then something would need to be done to get around the retrospective clause in the Act. On November 16 the Secretary of State for Scotland removed this impediment by announcing a further short bill which would enable Oscar Slater to appeal. The Bill went through both Houses on the nod and arrangements were put in hand for the appeal to be heard in the early summer of 1928.

Conan Doyle who had played such a large part in first securing the release of Slater and then in getting permission for the case to go to appeal now faced a personal problem. The appeal was going to cost a great deal of money and Slater had no funds of his own. If the appeal was won then there was a hope that costs would be awarded but this was by no means guaranteed. With no time available to organise any fund raising Conan Doyle generously agreed to underwrite the full cost of the appeal. It was a generous act for the costs were calculated to run into four figures.

The appeal of Oscar Slater opened at the High Court in Edinburgh on June 8, 1928, in the same room as the original trial and just a little more than nineteen years after the event. Unlike the original trial, however, there were now five judges sitting on the bench and the dock was empty. Slater, who was present, sat among the spectators. In spite of having put up the money for the show Doyle, who was also present, was granted no special privileges and he too was among the spectators. The appeal was led by Craigie Aitchison, K.C. who was assisted by Mr Clyde, Advocate. Clyde's father, Lord Clyde, The Lord Justice-General, as the senior judge led the bench.

The first day of the hearing was taken up with the setting out of the ground rules. The entire proceedings were, legally speaking, new territory with no precidents to guide the participants.

Aitchison requested permission to lead new evidence and to recall certain witnesses from the first trial. In particular it was requested that Helen Lambie should be re-called. As he told the court:—"According to our information, a week before the crime, Helen Lambie who was a maid in the service of Miss Gilchrist, went to see her former mistress, without any invitation and without any explanation as to why she had come. She had not seen the lady for three and a half years. She told her former mistress that there was strange goings on in the house of her mistress, that jewels were being secreted in strange places and that Miss Gilchrist had said that she was going to be murdered. In answer to a question by her former mistress as to whether anybody could gain admittance to the house while the maid was absent Helen replied that they could only do so if they knew the pre-arranged signal.

"A week after the crime Helen Lambie returned to the same lady; and on that occasion, being asked how the man who had committed the crime could have got access to the house, she did not answer the question, but volunteered the information, with great emphasis, that she would not know the man again; and on being pressed as to how the man got in, and on being reminded of her former statement, that he could only get in in accordance with a pre-arranged signal, she became agitated and denied that she had ever made such a statement, and she immediately left the house."

According to Aitchison this piece of *new* evidence could be corroborated by a solicitor who could tell the court that his client, the former mistress, had made a statement to him shortly after the murder of Miss Gilchrist. But what exactly could this solicitor tell the court? Nothing more than that the former mistress had made a statement to him. Whether the statement was true or nothing more that vapourings of a middle-aged woman he could have had no way of telling unless he, in fact, had been present at the interviews with Helen.

The former Mistress was, of course, Margaret Birrell although why Aitchison was so careful not to mention her name he does not tell us. But in any case the story of the first meeting, the one that took place before the murder was hardly new. Both Helen and Margaret Birrell had told Inspector Pyper all about it when he had first questioned them. Neither was the former mistress being entirely honest on other points when she discussed the matter later with her solicitor. It was not the case that Miss Birrell had never seen or spoken to her former maid during the three years which had elapsed since they had parted company. Margaret had seen Helen at Miss Gilchrist's house when she had called there a few weeks before the murder and presumably they had exchanged words on that occasion. She had also seen her on the Saturday before the murder when she had again called at the home of her aunt. It is also extremely unlikely that on other times when the niece had visited her aunt that Helen had been absent on every such occasion.

Helen had never denied that on the occasion of her admittedly surprised visit to her former mistress that she had mentioned Miss Gilchrist's fear of being robbed and possibly of being attacked. There was, remember, a spate of burglaries taking place in the area at that time and many of the elderly were frightened. She did deny however ever saying anything about the jewellery being hidden all over the house. That would have been palpably untrue as the jewellery had been hidden in the various items of clothing in the wardrobe and that was wild enough for anyone's money.

It is the second visit by Helen to her former employer that is infinitely more interesting. This visit was by invitation and its purpose, quite clearly, was to obtain from Helen a statement that she did not recognise the stranger in the hall as AB. After being subjected to what can only be described as some sharp cross-examination Helen, quite sensibly, left.

But in all honesty Margaret Birrell could not be described as clever. In a discussion between her and her former maid there can be no doubt who would have come out best. It is extremely unlikely then that Margaret initiated the meeting entirely on her own, someone must have told her what to say. It is also unlikely that having held the meeting Margaret would have had sufficient brains to have then gone to give her versions to a solicitor. My guess is that it was Sir William Burrell who set up the meeting and I would not have been surprised if the solicitor had been outside the door listening to what was being said. The whole episode smacks strongly of being an attempt to set up a defence of AB in advance of his being charged.

Among the new witnesses which the defence were hoping to call had been included the name of Oscar Slater on the grounds that he had not given evidence at the trial. The judges, however, were not prepared to accept this as the decision as to whether to take the stand or not had been one which had been entirely in the hands of the appellant and his advisers at the time. This refusal so upset Slater that he stormed out of the court declaring that the appeal was a farce and that he was abandoning it. For a few anxious hours it looked as though the proceedings would grind to a halt but better sense prevailed and Slater was persuaded to return to the court.

Legally speaking the judges could not be faulted for their decision but, in light of the other peculiar witnesses they were prepared to allow, it does seem curious that they chose to effectively silence the one person everybody wanted to hear. Having said this, however, I very much doubt whether his contribution would have been all that worthwhile unless the very questions that would have been of interest were allowed. And those questions, I suspect, would have been banned.

Among the more curious witnesses who were allowed to speak were William Roughhead and Mrs Adams, widow of Dr Adams. Mrs Adams, who had married the doctor in 1920 had not even known him at the time of the murder. Nevertheless she was permitted to tell the court what her late husband had allegedly told her about his theory of the chair having been used as the murder weapon. Similarly, William Roughhead was allowed to read out his preface to the book he had edited, The Trial of Oscar Slater. In this preface Roughhead outlines Adams theory of the chair. So in effect Roughhead was allowed to use his own words as being proof of what somebody else had said. In cross-examination, however, Roughhead had to admit that given the number of wounds and the weight of the chair then the theory did not seem all that tenable. His appearance in court, however, possibly did do his sales some good.

On July 20, after having heard all the arguments, the appeal judges delivered their verdict. The first question that they had to consider was whether the original verdict had been unreasonable and not supported by the evidence? In this the Law Lords had no doubt. In their opinion while it was possible to criticise much of the evidence, especially that concerned with identification, these criticisms had been made to the jury at the time and rightly or wrongly they had made up their own minds. This then was disallowed.

The second question the Law Lords had to consider was whether the new evidence that they had allowed was of such a nature that had it been given to the jury it would have affected their verdict? In their opinion it would not and so this part was also disallowed. With two strikes against him Slater must have already given up hope when the Law Lords turned to the third and final question.

At the trial the then Lord Advocate had made great use of the prisoner's admittedly bad background in order to further blacken the prisoner before the jury. And this in spite of the fact that the prisoner's character had not been an issue. In the opinion of Law Lords this had been quite permissable although perhaps regretable. What had not been permissible, however, was for the judge to take these admittedly true allegations and to use them in order to tell the jury that in the case of prisoners with such a bad character the presumption of innocence was not applicable. This, in the opinion of the Law Lords, ammounted to gross misdirection of the jury and consequently the verdict was set aside.

With the State now content to accept the verdict of the appeal court that Slater had been wrongfully imprisoned for nineteen years the question of compensation now arose. In Parliament, on July 23, the Secretary of State for Scotland announced that the Government was prepared to receive any claim that Slater might wish to submit. Slater replied through the press a few days later. "As far as I, Oscar Slater, am concerned, there will never be a bill for compensation sent in."

The Secretary of State, however, ignored this statement and on August 4 he wrote to Slater that the Lords of the Treasury, "have assented to an *ex gratia* payment to you of £6,000 in consequence of your wrongful conviction." He also asked how Slater wanted the money paid to him. Slater immediately replied that payment into his bank account would do nicely.

It might be thought that the use of the words 'wrongful conviction' implied a public recognition by the Secretary of State for Scotland that Slater was absolutely innocent of the crime for which he had spent so long in prison. Legally speaking Slater had been released because the procedure had erred thus making the question, as far as the law was concerned, of his actual guilt immaterial. Nevertheless, in the minds of the populace in general there existed little doubt that he had been declared innocent. In spite of his choice of phrase it would seem that the Secretary of State was also of this mind by his rather generous offer of compensation.

When the news broke that Slater had accepted the Government's offer of compensation a furious row broke out in the press. The cost of the appeal had been calculated at some £1,500 and Slater was making it quite clear that he had no intention of contributing a brass farthing towards it. A fund had been started, mainly among the Jewish community, which had raised some £700 leaving a shortfall to found of £800. As no one else was coming forward then it seemed that Conan Doyle would be stuck with the bulk of the bill.

Slater at the time, and still is, usually accused of behaving in an ungrateful manner towards those who had assisted him, especially Doyle. But how else should a pimp who had just done nineteen years in prison for a crime that nobody now believed that he had committed have been expected to act? What such commentators usually forget is that Slater had been required to find the whole cost of his original defence on his own. In any case Conan Doyle was not coming out of the affair without some advantage to himself. Over a number of years Conan Doyle had written numerous articles on Slater for which he had been well paid and this sum probably more than matched the loss that he made with respect to the cost of appeal. Further, in recent years his stock had taken something of a nose-dive following the publication of some photographs of fairies which he had authenticated. The Slater case returned to him some of his lost credibility.

The last word, however, must go to Helen Lambie.

Helen was at the time living in America although precisely when she went there is the cause of some confusion among her friends. In any case when the appeal court handed down its findings an enterprising reporter ran Helen to earth in Peoria, Illinois and got from her a statement. "I am glad that it is all over." Poor Helen, she better than most should have realised that murder never goes away.

CHAPTER 24

The five judges sitting as an appeal court might well have thought, as Helen hoped, that they had finally disposed of what was known as the Slater Case but if they did then they were indeed wrong. The problem was, of course, that they had found Slater innocent on a technicality while everybody else was now convinced that he had been innocent all along. If they were right then Slater's belated deliverance was really irrelevant to the central fascinating mystery, who then did kill Miss Gilchrist on that rainy December evening in Glasgow?

Although eighty years have now passed the story still gets its annual airing somewhere in the world and the questions raised are nearly always the same. Was the stranger in the hall the murderer? Why did the murderer wait until that particular, and not very convenient, moment to strike? What conceivable motive did the murderer have? Why was only one piece of jewellery stolen while other pieces were lying in full view? Why did Helen not do the most obvious thing and go straight into the sitting-room to first assure herself that her mistress was alright? Even more mysterious, why did she stand silent in the hall while the stranger made his exit?

These questions are some of the ones most asked by those with a keen, if amateurish, interest in the criminous. The more professional ask the technically more difficult questions. Why were there not more signs of blood, particularly transferred blood, as the murderer moved about the house? Why was the murderer apparently so relatively free from blood-stains. Arthur might not have seen the stains as the stranger passed by but he would have surely smelled the blood for it has a strong odour. What was the weapon used? All that is known is that it was small enough to be concealed on the person. What was to be deduced from the box of matches left behind? And possibly one of the most interesting questions of all, why was there blood on both sides of the impervious skin rug?

In fact, as you will now see, there was never really any mystery at all. Except, perhaps, how it was that Helen was able to get away with it when everything pointed towards her.

Helen Lambie was not wholly vindictive nor did she particularly dispise her mistress, her relationship with Miss Gilchrist was strictly one of servant to mistress. On the other hand Miss Gilchrist tended to regard her maid as being the faithful servant, a decent enough girl even if she was a bit stupid at times. In this attitude Miss Gilchrist was not alone, most employers regarded their servants as being loyal but stupid. In fact the first thing that any servant had to learn when entering service was how to appear stupid without actually being so. Nobody wanted a smart-arsed servant around.

Helen, as we know, had a weakness, she liked to dress herself up in her mistresses jewellery, especially on her evenings off. Up until a few weeks before the death the maid had been able to indulge her fancies for the jewellery was scattered about in the various pockets of the coats and dresses in the wardrobe and, of course, the wardrobe door was never locked. It was easy then to borrow one or two pieces provided that they were replaced in the morning before her mistress got up. But then Helen got careless and stopped replacing the jewellery promptly and Miss Gilchrist found out. By a stroke of good luck Mr Robertson had interceeded on her behalf but after that incident the wardrobe was always kept locked.

Ordinarily I suppose that Helen, after having had one close shave, should have recognised the foolishness of any further attempt to borrow the property of her mistress but the maid had of recent become a shade too bold for her own good. The thing was that Helen had acquired a boyfriend who had sufficient money to take her out to the more expensive places of entertainment to be found in Glasgow and the girl wanted to make a show. The jewellery made up for her lack of smart clothing although I suspect that she was also wearing some of her mistress's clothes as well.

Helen's gentleman friend was Patrick Nugent, a mature man of 40 years who had arrived in Scotland from Ireland as a young man and who had settled down in the small village of Carfin, near Motherwell. Motherwell, about fifteen miles from Glasgow, was at that time one of the world centres for the production of coal, iron and steel and was attracting migrants from as far away as the Baltic states. It was Patrick's boast in later life that when he arrived in Motherwell he had exactly 10d (4p) in his pocket.

Unlike many of his fellow countrymen Patrick was a man of sober and careful habits. Like many others he went at first down the pits but he saved his money and was soon able to establish himself as a street corner bookie. Of course such an occupation was illegal for off-course betting on horses and dogs except in certain circumstances was forbidden. But illegal or not there was never a time when every village did not have its street corner bookie plying his business in some close or pend strategically placed for a quick get away should the local constable appear. Compared with working down the pit the life of the bookie was considerably more healthy and certainly more lucrative in spite of the occasional brushes with the law. Patrick proved to be so successful at his calling that by 1908 he had a number of pitches in the various villages around Motherwell.

But the clamber up the greasy pole of success had not been an easy one. Success in any business endeavour is never without its difficulties and in the unregulated business of betting it was even more so. Competition tended to come in the form of large hard men and to hold on to a pitch a bookie had to be prepared from time to time to physically defend his interests. As bookies more often than not carried on their persons considerable sums of cash then they were also fair game for the mugger and other highwaymen. No bookie, then, could afford to step outside his house without having the comfort of some weapon such as cosh nestling in his pocket.

A big fish only because of the smallness of the pool Patrick was quite a celebrity in his world. The dream of most miners was always for his son to become a professional footballer and his daughter to marry the local bookmaker so that we may take it that Patrick never experienced any trouble normally in having his way with the local girls. Generally his problem would be in keeping them away. It must have come as something of a shock to him then when at a New Year dance in Wishaw, Helen rejected his advances. The fact that the first meeting took place on, as it were, neutral ground might help to explain one reason for the rejection. Patrick came from Carfin, an almost wholly catholic community, and less that a mile away from Holytown where Helen lived and which was almost wholly protestant. Thus although they lived almost next door to each other the difference in religion was so deep as to make it impossible for the couple ever to have met on their home ground.

With the ardour of which only a middle-aged man for a much younger girl can feel Patrick refused to take no for an answer. The rebuff only served to increase his determination which is probably the effect Helen intended from the beginning. By post and by emissary bearing gifts Patrick pressed forward with his suit all that winter and spring but it was not to be until the start of summer before she finally surrendered. In fact Patrick probably enjoyed the chase for he was something of a romantic at heart. Those who knew him tell me that he had a fine singing voice and always ready to oblige with an Irish love song.

Unfortunately none of the letters written by Patrick to Helen have survived but we do have some indication of the tone of their contents. When the police searched the house after the murder some of the letters were discovered and it was this that first brought Patrick to the attention of the police. From their line of questioning it is quite obvious that not only was Patrick declaring his undying love for Helen, he was also at the very least hinting at marriage. It was this hint at marriage that confused the police when they discovered that on November 26, 1908, Patrick had got himself married to another. Helen was asked if she was angry that a man who was declaring his love for her in no uncertain terms should suddenly take another. "No" Helen replied, "for marriage between us would have been impossible anyway. He is a catholic."

But I have run ahead of myself so I must return to the beginning of summer. Hardly had the romance got off to a start when the lovers found themselves temporarily parted. Every summer Miss Gilchrist took a house for the month at Girvan, a fishing port and holiday resort on the Clyde. It is interesting to note than on that year she also took on holiday with her Marion Ferguson, the girl she had named as the chief beneficiary in her will.

Clearly the thought of being parted from Helen for a whole month proved to be too much for Patrick and on one of the middle weekends he journeyed down to Girvan to see her. It was while he was there that he met Miss Gilchrist for the first time and possible the last time and he so charmed the old lady that she invited him to tea. Helen told her mistress that Patrick was a miner.

In the middle of September Miss Gilchrist went to stay with friends, the Fergusons, in Kilmarnock, a trip that entailed her staying overnight. Helen was left behind to look after the flat and the dog and she took advantage of her mistress's absence to invite Patrick to visit her. While in the house, apart from other things, Patrick was given a guided tour of the rooms and he took the opportunity to play a tune on the piano. One wonders what the professional musicians on the ground floor flat thought of his playing? He was also permitted to inspect and handle the collection of jewels which would seem to indicate that Helen could get into the wardrobe in spite of her mistress keeping a tight hold on the key. In fact it probably was not all that difficult for such locks were usually pretty easy to open.

Both Helen and Patrick when they spoke later of this visit claimed that the visit took place during the afternoon, a claim that I seriously beg to doubt. The truth of the matter is that if Patrick and Helen were not lovers before the visit then they certainly were after it.

Unless Helen had no previous sexual experience before the visit then the delights of love-making in bed must have come as something of a revelation to her. The normal love-making for a servant was fumbling and groping in some dark alley usually while standing in a pool of stinking water. One thing is fairly certain and that is that after that day Helen was determined that in the future all her love-making would be carried out in comfort.

To smuggle Patrick into the house while Miss Gilchrist was present was ridiculously easy. Miss Gilchrist was receiving medication from her doctor and a reasonable assumption would be that a little something to make her sleep at night was included among the medicants. But if even if they were not included, sleeping draughts were readily available without prescription at any chemist shop. Thus on the nights that Helen wished to bring Patrick into the house all she had to do was to make sure that her mistress received an extra heavy dose of a sleeping draught before going to bed.

There was only one real problem and that was the small dog. I fear that on the first September visit some of the romance of the moment was spoiled by the dog barking and scratching at the bedroom door. There was no other way, the dog simply had to go and this was achieved by giving it poison in its food.

In order for Patrick to get married on November 26 then notice of the marriage would have to be made at the latest by November 4. As we know that the love affair between Patrick and Helen was at least still on at the end of September and the beginning of October then there was hardly sufficient time for the couple to part and for Patrick to take another on the rebound. A more likely explanation would be that while Patrick was initially pursuing Helen he was also having an affair with another girl who became pregnant. Given the choice it is obvious that Patrick would have preferred to buy off the first girl had he been able to get Helen. But Helen had no intention of marrying nor had she any intention of giving up her lover. As far as she was concerned she was quite content to be the mistress in Glasgow and to leave another to sit by the fire waiting for the husband to come home.

Both Helen and Patrick claimed that by October they had parted but as we shall see those who were asking the questions did not believe this answer.

CHAPTER 25

The disaster came one morning early in December when Helen discovered that she had lost the gold crescent brooch with its single row of diamonds. The night previous she had been out with Patrick and as usual she had been wearing some of her mistress's jewellery. Either the clasp had been loose or she had been careless in fastening it but whatever the reason the consequences were all too obvious. There was little point in calling on the police just in case an honest citizen had found the brooch and handed it in. She might just as well make a confession. The police, who were not complete fools in such matters, would be hardly likely to believe that a servant girl could own such an expensive piece of jewellery. Even if the brooch had been handed in there was no way by which she could claim it back without the truth coming out. There was seemingly no escape for Helen and the prospect of prison must have appeared inevitable. Courts were especially hard on servants who stole from their mistresses.

Almost certainly it was the spate of recent burglaries that first planted the idea in Helen's mind that there might be a way out of her difficulties. If only the burglars would rob Miss Gilchrist's flat then the missing brooch could be passed off as being part of the loot. The question was how, then, could one persuade the burglars to rob Miss Gilchrist?

From the initial thought the next step was obvious. If there was no way to get the burglars to rob the house then why not stage the burglary herself? The end result would be the same and the burglars would get the blame. But while the idea seemed foolproof the technicalities of staging such a burglary, especially to an amateur, must have seemed unsurmountable. Miss Gilchrist had of recent become very security conscious and the three locks on the front door were always locked every night. Trying to force the front door then would create such a noise as to not only wake up her mistress but to possibly wake up the neighbours also. A straight-forward burglary, then, would be difficult if not impossible.

Strangely the idea of having the robbery staged on a Sunday morning when both her mistress and her neighbours would be out at church never seems to have crossed her mind although the house would be empty for some two hours.

The possibility that killing her mistress as a solution probably came to Helen after the visit of Alexander and Margaret Birrell to their aunt. The appearance of Alexander in itself must have intrigued Helen for this was the only occasion on which he had called on his aunt during the entire three years that Helen had been working at the flat. The novelty itself would have been more than a sufficient inducement to Helen to listen at the door of the sittingroom to find out the cause. In the event she did not even have to listen at the door for the visit rapidy developed into an acrimonious argument over money and voices were raised.

Later, long after the couple had departed, it must have struck Helen. that she had missed a glorious opportunity. She could have battered her mistress to death the moment that the nephew and niece had left. Given the argument over money that had taken place then Helen could have killed the old lady and blamed it on the nephew and niece. No one would ever have thought that their accuser was the guilty person. No servant was that bright and in any case what possible motive would the maid have had for doing such a thing? Even when the brooch would be found to be missing the age of the old lady would leave the heirs to suppose that she had probably lost it. It was the kind of wild plan which might have succeeded.

Helen was not a vicious girl, it was just that she was in a terrible jamb. She knew that two or three years in prison, even if it didn't break her, would ruin the rest of her life completely. On the other hand her mistress was old and liable to die at any minute. To kill her then might only be to rob her of a few days of life. Weighed in the balance the scales came down heavily against Marion Gilchrist.

The final plan to solve her problem, once arrived at, would be maintained almost without change right to the bitter end. Helen's strength lay in her ability to plan in detail, her weakness was a reluctance to change. Both traits may be seen in her plan. She would, she decided, murder her mistress and protect herself by constructing an alibi, but for the alibi she would require an accomplice. The help of Patrick would be required.

We can only guess at the arguments Helen used to persuade Patrick, but arguments there must have been before her lover agreed to offer his neck to the noose. One possible argument she could have used would have been the threat. If the missing brooch ever became a police matter then Patrick himself would also be a suspect. By the nature of their calling bookies were regarded as being, if not criminals themselves, then at least the associates of criminals. If Helen could not persuade the police that she had acted entirely on her own, and she could hint that she doubted the strength of her own powers of persuasion, then Patrick might easily end up spending more time in jail for the missing brooch than she.

There was, however, a reward to sweeten the threat. After the excitement had died down the jewellery could be sold and the proceeds used to set up Helen in a flat to which Patrick would have a front door key.

What Helen proposed to do was to kill her mistress and then admit Patrick to the flat. She would then leave, ostensibly to go a message for her mistress and during the time that she was away Patrick could stage the robbery. If say she went to buy an evening paper and left at seven o'clock she could extend the time out of the house by saying that she had to wait for the final edition to be delivered. By this means Patrick would have more than fifteen minutes to carry out his part of the plan. On her return Patrick could either strike her a blow with the cosh or with his fist, it didn't matter which just as long as there was a visible sign of an injury. Helen would then freign unconsciousness giving Patrick sufficient time to clear the district before she raised the alarm.

The major weakness of the plan was how to explain away the presence of a stranger in the house short of breaking down the door. The police would hardly be likely to swallow the story that Miss Gilchrist admitted a stranger when she was alone in the house. But Helen had an answer to that problem. She would say that although the hall had been dark when she returned she neverthless had a distinct impression that the man who had struck her down had been Alexander Birrell. Nothing positive, just an impression. Once the police learned of the row over money they could be depended upon to draw the proper conculsions.

It was to this end that Helen took the first step in her plan when shortly before the murder she called on her former employer, Margaret Birrell. While there she spoke of her mistress's fear of being burgled and perhaps of even being attacked in the process. This would then look later that it had been the visit and the subject discussed that had given Margaret and her brother the idea of robbing and killing their aunt. I suspect, although Margaret does not mention it, that it was also at Helen's suggestion that Margaret called on her aunt two days before the murder in order to bury their differences. The real purpose of the visit was to make it appear that the niece was 'casing the joint' prior to the murder.

During that visit I also suspect that Margaret admitted that she was there at the suggestion of Helen. This would account for Miss Gilchrist's fulsome praise for her maid.

On the day before the murder, Sunday afternoon, Helen had the afternoon off and she was out of the flat until shortly after 6pm. Strangely enough while she admits to being out she does not say where she was although the number of places one could go on a

Sunday afternoon in Glasgow was limited. The reason for her reticence was that she was meeting Patrick for a last minute check on the plans and probably to receive the cosh which he had brought for her and which would be used as the murder weapon. With only 24 hours to go then both of them must have been in a high state of excitment and it would not be surprising if Helen suggested to Patrick that he should at least spend some part of the night if not the whole night with her.

As Patrick could not be admitted to the house until Miss Gilchrist was safely tucked up in bed he had, perforce, to hang about in the street until it was safe for him to enter. It was while he was hanging around that he was seen by at least two and possibly three witnesses. Two of these witnesses, as you will recall, a cabinet-maker and a grocer, claimed to have seen him at different times, 6.45pm and nine o'clock and although they give different descriptions they are clearly talking about the same man for they both significantly say that the man they saw looked as though he was either waiting for someone or something. The third witness, Dr Adams, gives yet another description but he too says that the man looked as though he was waiting for someone, possibly a maid from one of the houses.

On her return to the flat, Helen had to prepare and serve supper and then to persuade her mistress that it was time to go to bed. The signs are that Miss Gilchrist was in no hurry to retire and she took her time about it. As a counter measure Helen was more than liberal with the sleeping draught and as a consequence her mistress was still so woozy the next morning that she lay on in bed until beyond noon.

CHAPTER 26

At about 9am on the morning of her death Miss Gilchrist was served her breakfast in bed. Shortly after mid-day she rose, had lunch and then at around 2pm she went out to pay some bills. One of the bills which she had paid was her rent and she took the opportunity to complain about the flat above still being empty. One can understand her concern for with winter now on there was always the risk of frozen and burst water pipes. She was out for little more than two hours returning at about 4.30 when she surprised Helen entertaining another maid to afternoon tea. If she had had any objections to her maid entertaining then she certainly did not mouth them, she contented herself with merely putting her head into the kitchen before retiring to her sitting-room. A few minutes after this the visitor left and so the last independent evidence we have of Miss Gilchrist being alive is timed at being 4.30 in the afternoon. Beyond this time we have only Helen's version and as we shall now see that version is hardly accurate.

In 1908, just as today, most of the citizens of Glasgow dined betwen six and seven in the evening although with people working longer hours in those days it was probably nearer seven than six. Only a very few with pretensions to being superior sat down to table at a later hour. Indeed one of the social changes which Miss Gilchrist had witnessed in her long life had been the gradual pushing back of the time for the main meal from 4pm until six. Thus we are intitled to assume that as a normal practice Miss Gilchrist tended to dine early rather than late. This assumption would seem to be bourne out by Helen who claimed that it had been her intention to go shopping after she had returned from buying the evening paper which would suggest that her Mistress had already dined. If not then Miss Gilchrist would be intending to dine at about 9pm which is plainly ridiculous.

The digestive system is a rather remarkable clock in as much as it takes the food we eat some 12 hours to be completely digested. What is more the rate of digestion is linear, that is to say that after approximately six hours the food is half digested, and so on. Best of all when you die the digestive process ceases almost immediately so that if the time of the last meal is known then from the degree of digestion the time of death may be quite accurately fixed.

Interestingly enough just a few months before the death of Miss Gilchrist the newspapers had been full of a rather brutal murder which hinged around this very point. Georgina Moore, a young girl, had apparently been abducted as she returned to school after lunch, taken some forty miles and then murdered and her body thrown into a river where she was not found until five days later. The lover of the child's father, Ester Pay, was arrested and tried for the crime and the prosecution looked very strong against her. She was, however acquited after it was shown that the child must have been killed shortly after she had eaten her lunch, the lunch had hardly started to be digested, and the case against Mrs Pay rested on the child still being alive at seven o'clock in the evening. This evidence incidentally was given by the doctor who was acting for the prosecution.

As a pathologist of some note and experience Professor Glaister must have been aware of the Georgina Moore case, unlike most murders it had made the pages of the better papers, and as it had only occured a few months before the death of Miss Gilchrist it must have been still fresh in his memory. It is strange then that the warning bells did not start ringing when he noted the stomach contents of the dead woman. In his report Glaister quite clearly states that he noted the presence of 'partly digested food' which could only indicate to the trained observer that Miss Gilchrist had eaten her last meal at least some three hours before she died. If then she had died at seven o'clock then she had died without the benefit of her last meal for what Glaister was looking at was undoubtedly the remnants of her lunch and breakfast. Even more telling, had Miss Gilchrist died at seven o'clock then that would have been six hours after her lunch and consequently the food in the stomach would not have been partially digested but half digested. On the evidence of her stomach Miss Gilchrist had probably been killed at least two hours earlier, at around five o'clock.

Although there is other evidence which tends to show that Miss Gilchrist was killed much earlier than is generally imagined and also that the murder did not take place in the sitting-room, I will not at this point go any further into it. Instead, for the sake of narrative, I will assume that this is the case and offer the proof when it naturally occurs.

When her visitor had departed Helen immediately set to to prepare for the murder. In the sitting-room her victim sat quietly at the table next to the fire reading her magazine. Helen had sense enough to realise the possibility of there being a considerable quantity of blood spilled and accordingly she made her preparations. Her normal work day dress was removed and replaced with an old dress which could be burned in the kitchen fire later. There was also the possibility of there being noise, sufficient noise as Miss Gilchrist slumped to the floor to alarm anyone in the kitchen of the flat below and to bring them up to the door to inquire. If this happened it was her intention to say that the noise they heard was that of the pulley falling. As a further precaution, and to some extent as part of the trap as well, Helen turned down the gas light. From some of the back windows in Grant Street it was possible to look out over the back court and to see into the kitchen, more especially at night time when it was dark and the kitchen was illuminated by the gas light.

Helen knew that sooner or later her mistress would come into the kitchen. It might be because being old-fashioned her mistress liked to supervise the preparation of the evening meal. On the other hand it might be because her maid had not replied to the summons of the bell telling her that her mistress required her. It might be that Miss Gilchrist might have suddenly realised that there was no sound from the kitchen. Whatever the reason all that Helen would have to do would be to sit tight and sooner rather than later her mistress would come to her.

From the way the kitchen door was hung (see layout) then anyone standing behind it would be hidden from the sight of the person entering until that person had advanced into the centre of the room. Helen took up such a position and waited. The trap worked and Miss Gilchrist finally came through to the kitchen and as she opened the kitchen door the fact that the room was almost in darkness must have alarmed the old woman. Nevertheless, Miss Gilchrist advanced into the kitchen and as she came into view Helen stepped from her place of concealment and struck her a savage blow on the back of the head. Without uttering a sound Miss Gilchrist slumped to the floor unconcious.

Quite ruthlessly Helen now turned the old lady over on to her back and kneeling at the right side of her head she struck her mistress another savage blow of such ferocity to the left eye that the eyeball was driven through the shattered bone of the orbit into the brain. Rather surprisingly Glaister, who should have known better, assumed that this blow had been delivered while Miss Gilchrist had been standing upright and conscious. This of course is plainly ludicrous for in such circumstances the victim could be expected to take some kind of evasive action even if it was only reflexive. But even if not then the blow would have certainly caused the head to rotate thus reducing some of the force. To penetrate the thick wall of the orbit the head had to be firmly supported such as if the body was lying on the floor.

In spite of the large hole in the brain cavity the dead woman probably did not bleed all that much. The initial blow to the head could have been expected to produce a state of shock and the blood pressure to plummet. What mess there was was quickly cleared up and the rags and the dress burned in the fire. All Helen had to do now was to wait for the arrival of Patrick and the second stage of the plan. But the thought of sitting for some two hours in the kitchen with the face of the dead woman exposed clearly proved to be too much for Helen. Going through to the sitting-room she lifted the skin rug and carrying it back to the kitchen placed it over the head of her mistress.

Women and men do not think in the same way, what is logical to a woman is not necessarily so to a man and vice versa. This difference in thinking has been the cause of a great deal of unhappiness in the world. When Helen carried the rug back through and placed it on the head of Miss Gilchrist she might not have been concious of it but she was in fact making an important decision. Unavoidably the rug would be stained. The question then was, which side? To any female the answer would be obvious. If the rug had to be stained then better it should be that the stain should be on the underside where it would not matter. Helen, then, placed the rug over the head with the underside next to the wound.

Right on cue Patrick arrived at the door to the close at a few minutes to seven o'clock but unfortunately so did Rowena Liddell and Rowena had a good look at him. But Rowena also did something else which somehow was never given the importance which it deserved. After entering her mother's house Rowena, almost immediately, came back out again to have a second look but the man had vanished. Now the time lapse between entering her mother's house and coming back out could only have been a few seconds, she had clearly got no further than over the threshold, not long enough for the man to have walked into another street out of sight. Nor was there sufficient time for him to have rung the door bell of any of the adjacent houses and to have been admitted. The only place he could have disappeared into was Miss Gilchrist's close and the door to that close must have been opened by prior arrangement and not by the ringing of the bell for Arthur would have undoubtedly heard the bell and he says that he did not.

Once in the flat Helen and Patrick had to move fast and Helen again turned down the gas light in the kitchen least they be seen. With Patrick lifting at the heavy end, the head, and Helen at the feet they carried the body through to the sitting-room. As a gentleman Patrick went first walking backwards and he kept on walking until his feet came into contact with the fender of the fire. Patrick was forty years of age, inclined to stoutness and probably a bit stiff in the joints. Thus instead of bending straight down to place the body on the floor he canted the body to the right. As he did so the right arm fell away while the left arm pressed tight against the body. At the same time the twisting body caused Helen to let the left foot cross the right. The body was later noted to be lying with the limbs fully extended, the right arm at right angles and the left foot over the right. The whole picture cried out that the body had not fallen on the spot but that it had been carefully laid down. The gap between the head and fender was two feet, just sufficient distance for someone to have stood between the head and the fender. The feet were pointing directly at the door. Helen being able to see where she was going, was able to walk in a staight line from the door.

The accepted version of the attack offered by Glaister was never challenged in the court and yet obviously it could not have been correct. According to Glaister Miss Gilchrist, while standing facing her attacker, had been struck first a blow to the left-hand side of her face, a blow which could reasonably have been expected to have caused the head to rotate violently to the right. When Helen had struck her first blow to the back of the head Miss Gilchrist's upper dentures had fallen out of her mouth to the floor. Ever careful, when Helen had carried the body through to the sitting-room she brought with her the half set of dentures and dropped them onto the floor near to the head. She made a mistake however for she dropped the dentures to the wrong side. Later they were found lying some three or four feet from the left-hand side of the head.

Had it been as Glaister had told it then the false teeth should have finished up either on the table or beyond and certainly to the right of the body.

When a dead body is moved then quite often the movement causes an involuntary movement in one of the limbs or for stomach gas to be released. This is common enough for it to form the basis for many funny stories told by the undertaking fraternity, the newcommer immediately thinks that the corpse is not quite dead. Something like this must have happened after Helen and Patrick moved the body of Miss Gilchrist and they too thought that the old lady was not quite dead.

With little time left if she was to construct her alibi Helen handed over the task of finishing the job off to Patrick, a task for which he clearly had little stomach. The skin rug had been brought back through with the body and lifting it Patrick placed it over the old woman's head so that he would not have to view the consequences of his actions. Like Helen before him although he did not realise it he too was having to make a choice and to the problem he brought male logic. To a man the upper side of the rug, the side that comes into contact with the soles of the shoes, is the bit which is designed for coming into contact with the dirt. Consequently Patrick placed the upper side of the rug against the head and that is how the rug came to be stained on both sides.

Unlike manufactured rugs which are quite flexible the skin rug is inclined to be stiff. It is about as stiff as a piece of thin cardboard and when laid over the head it protruded beyond it rather than following the contours. Thus instead of acting as a barrier to the flying pieces of tissue and blood it behaved more like a funnel directing the material over a restricted arc. Glaister would later note that such had been the ferocity of this second attack that pieces of blood and tissue were found to be not only sticking to the iron bars of the fire-nest but also to the bricks surrounding the fire-nest.

The open coal fire has many attractions but its drawback is that it requires a great deal of attention. Periodically the ash has to be scraped out and of course fresh coal has to be added every couple or so hours or the fire will go out.

Monday, December 21, had been a typical winter's day for Glasgow and Miss Gilchrist was no doubt pleased when she returned from paying her bills that she did so to a good fire in the sitting-toom. But as the minutes ticked away that fire must have been slowly burning down and indeed it might have been that very fact which led her first to try and summons her maid and when she got no response to go through to the kitchen to find out what the matter was. After Miss Gilchrist had been killed then apart from going to collect the skin rug Helen had no reason to go back into the sitting-room and so the fire died out.

Blood and tissue consist of water, protein and hydrocarbons, all of which are destroyed when subjected to temperatures above 100°C and the iron bars of a good fire have a temperature considerably more than that. As children we used to have fun dropping water onto the iron bars of the fire and watching the droplets hiss and dance to the heat. Glaister's behaviour might have been somewhat less than might have been expected but when he noted blood and tissue on the iron bars and the bricks that is what he saw. Had he noted only stains then he would gave said 'stains indicative of blood and tissue'. Clearly then not only had the fire gone out but it had been out long enough so that by seven o'clock the iron bars were cool enough to do no damage to the blood and tissue.

The only explanation which would account for the fire in the sitting-room being out, or nearly out, by seven o'clock has to be that Miss Gilchrist had been dead for some considerable time before seven o'clock.

CHAPTER 27

Arthur Adams had been alarmed when he heard the distinct sound of someone rapping on the floor above. He assumed that the noise had been made by his elderly neighbour but more than likely what he heard was Patrick occasionally missing the head of his victim and the cosh striking the floor.

When Arthur arrived at the front door of his neighbour's flat and rang the door-bell Patrick must have still been in the sitting-room. Glaister guessed that the second attack must have lasted for some five minutes which was probably an exageration but the attack certainly did take an appreciable time. The sound of the door-bell must have sounded to Patrick like the prison bell which was traditionally tolled on the morning of an execution. He could only have been greatly relieved when the door-bell stopped ringing and he heard the sound of footsteps receding down the stairs. The visitor, whoever he or she was, had not bothered to stay long.

By the time that Arthur had returned a few minutes later Patrick was quite definitely out of the sitting-room and in the bedroom. The hall was lit and although it was not possible to see clearly through the blue tinted side-lights any figure crossing the hall would have been seen. This time Arthur was more determined and he rang the door-bell furiously. Although he does not say so it is reasonable to suppose that he also shouted through the letter-box. Thus inside the bedroom Patrick would have been aware that it was a man who was outside although the knowledge could have done him little immediate good. After all he was trapped in the house and could no more reach Arthur then Arthur could reach him.

Helen showed remarkable presence of mind when she returned to find Arthur on the door-step. Falling back on the story she had rehearsed for just this contingency, although perhaps later than she had anticipated, she told Arthur that noise he had heard was probably that of the pulley falling down. This of course ignored the fact that the noise Arthur had heard had been from the room immediately above while the pulley was located in the kitchen. But Helen was always loath to give up a good story.

One thing did strike Arthur as being rather peculiar, that was although apparently calm, Helen persisted in speaking in a loud voice. It never did dawn on him, or anyone else for that matter, that by speaking in a loud voice Patrick could hear every word she was saying. He heard Helen quite clearly telling Arthur about the pulley and from what she was saying he correctly guessed that it was her intention to lure Arthur into the kitchen and so provide him with a clear escape route. The only problem was that while Patrick fully understood her intention Arthur completely failed to do so and so as Helen advanced into the hall Arthur obstinately remained standing in the door-way.

When Helen had got as far as the entrance to the short lobby leading to the kitchen it seems that she then realised that Arthur was not following her so she stopped and glanced over her left shoulder in the direction of the front door. In the bedroom Patrick waited, Helen had stopped speaking so that he really had no idea where either she or Arthur were. Finally, assuming that they had in fact reached the kitchen, Patrick opened the bedroom door and stepped briskly into the hall. Like a truck free-wheeling down hill out of control Patrick saw Arthur standing in the door-way but he could do nothing to stop. For a moment it must have seemed as though collision was unavoidable and then, at the last moment, Arthur stepped aside. Two steps from the door took Patrick on to the stairs and liberty.

Later Arthur would be persuaded that Helen had stopped when she heard the bedroom door opening and that she had turned to take a view of the stranger. But the stranger was to her right and yet she turned left. It was Arthur she was looking at.

Helen had been metriculous in her planning so that it is hardly likely that she had forgotten to plan the escape route but what that route was we may only guess. The only thing that is certain is that Patrick, on gaining the street, did not turn right and head towards St Georges Road. That was the direction that Arthur took in pursuit and he saw no sign of the stranger. I suspect that the reason he set off in that direction was that Helen had suggested it.

For what it is worth I am of the opinion that on leaving the close Patrick left inclined across West Princes Street and entered Queens Crescent. That would be the quickest way of disappearing from anyone who might follow him down stairs. From Queens Crescent it was only a short step to the anonymity of Great Western Road. Once there he almost certainly turned left and walked westward to the first tram stop. He could then travel by tram for about a mile to Byres Road and hence by other tram to Argyle Street. From there he could easily make his way to the city centre and transport home to Motherwell. Thus while Arthur pursued eastwards Patrick escaped westwards.

CHAPTER 28

If only Pyper had had his wits about him he could have solved the case within a couple of hours of his arrival at the scene of the crime. Within that short space of time he was presented with three clues which, had they been followed, would have told him who killed Marion Gilchrist. The first of these clues might be reasonably described as 'The Mystery of the Missing Newspaper'.

In fairness to Pyper it has to be said that Helen's actions on entering the flat on her return did strike him as being decidedly odd as indeed it has so struck everyone else who has since written about the mystery. In spite of the fact that Arthur has been violently ringing the door-bell and banging just as violently on the door—both actions guaranteed to strike terror into the heart of the old lady occupying the house—Helen made no attempt to first reassure her mistress. When Helen was later questioned about this she excused her action on the grounds that Arthur was going on so that she became flustered and could only think of putting his mind at rest first. As by this time Pyper had spoken to Arthur and had probably already come to the opinion that the neighbour was something of an old woman then the excuse seemed reasonable.

One of the first things that Pyper did on his arrival was to make an accurate list of all the visible contents of the sitting-room and the bedroom. For instance in the list concerned with the sitting-room it was noted that the table was covered with a cloth and that on the cloth was lying an open magazine and a pair of gold-rimmed spectacles. There is, however, no mention of the newspaper that Helen had purchased although, surprisingly, the halfpenny change from the purchase was lying on the table. Likewise the list concerned with the bedroom makes no mention of the newspaper. From this we may only conclude, unless Helen carried the newspaper with her for the rest of the night, that she had in fact laid the newspaper down in the kitchen.

In the panic of the moment it would be perfectly understandable that Helen, on entering the kitchen, should have laid down the newspaper. After all she was carrying it in her hand and at such a time one would wish one's hands to be free. But the halfpenny change was something entirely different. Two or three minutes later Helen would be standing in the sitting-room looking down at the body of her dead mistress and she would claim that the sight transfixed her to the spot. But this could only have been temporary for before going out of the room to tell Arthur the shocking news she carefully stepped round the body and deliberately laid the halfpenny change on the table.

Now why did she do that? It could hardly have been honesty for the change did not belong to her mistress. Miss Gilchrist had been dead for a couple of hours before Helen went out to buy the newspaper and Helen had paid for the paper out of her own pocket. In any case why had Helen offered the newsagent a penny for a paper which only cost a halfpenny?

In 1908 the halfpenny was the most popular coin in circulation, there were more items on sale for a halfpenny than a penny. By far the most of the revenue taken by the transport and gas utilities were taken in halfpennies. You could insure yourself for a halfpenny per week. Five woodbines, a box of matches, a cup of tea all cost a halfpenny. Such was the demand and usage of the coin that it would be a rare invididual who did not have a halfpenny on her or his person at any given moment.

Helen was the mistress of detailed planning and if she tendered a penny for a paper which only cost a halfpenny then it had to have some significance. Although it can only be a guess I suspect that the intention was that Patrick, when he left the flat, should take with him the copy of the newspaper. The suggestion would be that he did so in order to wrap up the murder weapon and so the police would be looking for a man carring a rolled-up newspaper. As Patrick would be carrying the paper folded up in his pocket then few would remember him. It would also give the impression that the weapon was probably soaked in blood where as in fact Helen had more than sufficient time to have washed it clean.

But the only proof that the police would initially have, until they could get around to interviewing the newsagent, that Helen had actually purchased a paper was if there was change from the transaction. In the event things did not work out as planned and Helen still had the newspaper when Patrick left but that was purely accidental.

Whether in fact Pyper ever saw the newspaper is open to question for if he did he failed to record it. He did, however, note the presence of the halfpenny on the table in the sitting-room and identified it quite clearly as being the change from the purchase of the newspaper. As it was the next morning before the newsagent was interviewed then for the first twelve or so hours the halfpenny did after all serve to confirm the reason for Helen's absence from the flat. It was the proof she had actually bought a newspaper.

The second mystery may rightfully be called The Mystery of the Three Keys.

The handbag belonging to Miss Gilchrist was also searched and among the contents were noted three keys. As the front door had three locks and as each required its separate key then the obvious conculsion might well have been that the keys were the keys to the front door. But in this case the obvious is not correct for the keys had nothing to do with the door, for a start they were too small.

Although we are not told what locks the keys belonged to there is sufficient evidence elsewhere to throw some light on the mystery. As Miss Gilchrist a short time before her death had taken to keeping the key to the wardrobe in her possession at all times then one of the keys found undoubtedly must have fitted the lock to the wardrobe. There was also a safe or strongbox which was kept in the sideboard and which, incidentally, for an excellent reason was never made public. If its existence had been generally known then it would have completely contradicted the story, a story which the police apparently were quite happy to keep in circulation, that the dead woman had been keeping secret papers in a flimsy wooden box in the spare room. The second key then, undoubtedly, fitted the lock on the strongbox.

As the police hinted, although without ever offering proof, that the wooden box in the bedroom also had a lock fitted to it then a reasonable guess would be that the third key fitted this lock.

The significance of the three keys, however, lies not in the fact that they were found but in the fact that, search as much as Pyper might, they were the only keys to be found in the presence of the dead woman. The assumption that first night that Pyper was making was that Miss Gilchrist had admitted her assailent. But was Miss Gilchrist likely to have admitted someone and them immediately taken the keys she had used to unlock the front door and hide them somewhere else in the flat other than the sitting-room, bedroom or kitchen? Of course she would not, what conceivable reason could she have had for doing such a thing? In any case Arthur heard the noise of the attack almost immediately after it was known that Helen had left the house. Miss Gilchrist simply did not have the time to hide the keys even if she had wished to.

The only reasonable conculsion to be drawn from the fact that Miss Gilchrist was without the means to admit her assailant is that she did not do so. And if she did not admit him then only Helen could have done so.

The third mystery is The Mystery of the Box of Matches.

On entering the bedroom the first thing that Patrick had to do was to light the gas so that he could see what he was doing. This was a two handed job, one hand to hold the match and the other to turn the valve to the open position. As a consequence having struck the match he laid the box down and in the excitement that followed he forgot to pick it back up again. That box of Runaway matches was to prove to be the only tangible proof of Patrick's presence in the flat to be found.

Matches are a unique commodity in as much as there is no such thing as a bad match sold in Britain and they are all sold at the same price. In the market place no manufacturer has an advantage in quality or price. Nevertheless every brand of match has remarkable customer loyalty. For instance if you walk into a shop in Glasgow and ask merely for a box of matches you will be automatically served with either a box of Vulcan or Bluebell matches. Similarly, the safety match, which enjoys a wide sale in other parts of the country, cannot be sold in Scotland. Here we seemingly remain stubbornly wedded to the notion that a match which does not require a strip of sandpaper to be stuck to the box is not a match at all.

In Edwardian times there were of course far more brands of matches on sale than there are today and many matches were used as mediums for advertising and as lost leaders. Public houses and tobacco shops often gave away matches on request, the cost being carried by the advertiser.

Bryant & May produced Runaway matches at their Maryhill factory about a mile distance from where Miss Gilchrist lived. The brand, however, as Pyper very quickly learned was not one which sold particulary well in Glasgow. What little sale for the brand there was tended to be confined to the cheaper retail shops who used the brand as a lost leader. But Bryant & May were not in the business of producing matches for fun. If they were prepared to go to some length to produce a particular brand then you may take that if it did not sell in one area then it most certainly did well in some other area. If Runaway did not sell in Glasgow then they were selling somewhere else.

Inspector Pyper completely failed to recognise the importance of the box of Runaway matches as a clue. Indeed he admits that the moment he discovered that they did not sell in Glasgow then he ceased to have any further interest in them. But what if they had been a popular brand? A brand to be found in the pockets of every male in the streets? What would that have told him? Nothing more than that the stranger probably came from the city. Just the same as the fact they were not a popular brand should have told him that it was extremely likely that the stranger came from out of town.

Within two hours of his arrival at the scene of the crime Pyper had the solution to the murder in his hands. He had evidence from her behaviour that Helen knew that her mistress was dead before she entered the flat on her return from the newsagent. From the missing keys he had the evidence that only Helen could have admitted the stranger into the flat, only she had the means. Finally from the matchbox he had a clear indication of the strong probability that the stranger, like Helen, came from out of town. The only thing he lacked was the wit and the will to recognise what he had. Is it any wonder then that Helen and Patrick walked free while an innocent man went to prison for their crime.

CHAPTER 29

To most writers on the murder of Marion Gilchrist it is generally held that the role played by Oscar Slater in the affair was the consequence of a ghastly mistake. Perhaps Detective John Trench expressed the notion best when he remarked in his evidence to the Secret Inquiry, "if only the police had got to him (Slater) before he left Glasgow then he would have been quickly eliminated from any further inquiry." What Trench, of course was saying was that it was the unhappy conjunction of Slater's departure from Glasgow with the desire of the police to interview him which gave credence to the assumption that he was fleeing from justice.

The accident theory, however, gives rise to as many questions as it provides answers. For instance why did the police fail to establish contact with Slater before he left the city? It was not after all the case that he had not been available. Slater did not leave his flat until after 8pm that Friday evening and yet from 7pm until 7.45pm a detective called Powell sat in the flat immediately below Slater's interviewing a Mrs Bernstein, a neighbour. Even more surprising apparently Powell had been sent to 69 St Georges Road for the express purpose of interviewing Slater and yet at no time did he make any attempt to climb the flight of stairs and ring Slater's doorbell. Perhaps most surprising of all, however, was that later when the truth came out, that Slater had still been present in his house, not one word of criticism was ever leveled at Powell by any of his superiors and yet on the face of it he was guilty of gross deriliction of his duty.

It is amusing to reflect on the fact that had Powell only remained for another 15 minutes in the neighbour's house he would have been an eyewitness to Slater's departure.

There is also the very peculiar attitude, one might almost say childlike stubborness, shown by Superintendent Ord in his refusal to accept the overwhelming evidence that not only had Slater travelled to Liverpool instead of London but that it had been his intention to do so from the very beginning. Even five months after the event, during the trial, Ord was still claiming that Slater had bought two tickets to London in order to throw the police off his track.

A major mystery has to be why did Oscar Slater, a traveller of some experience, choose to travel by the 9.05pm train, the least suitable of all the trains available that day? To travel by the 9.05, essentially a milk train which stopped at almost every halt on the way, entailed a night journey of some seven hours and which at that time of the year was something to be avoided. What is even worse on arrival at Liverpool the couple would be faced with the choice of either spending the last few hours of the night in a station waiting-room or else paying a full night's tariff for a hotel room which they would only occupy for three or four hours.

If we know anything at all about Slater that is that he was a man who liked to get value for money, almost obsessively so. All his palaver with Thomas Cook & Son about booking his cabin did pay off in the end. By refusing to book in Glasgow and electing instead to wait until he got to Liverpool, Slater was able to secure an outside cabin for the same price as an inside one. He saved £4 on the deal.

On that particular day, in spite of it being a holiday, Slater had quite a wide choice of trains to Liverpool. The 10.10 arriving Liverpool shortly after 2pm; the 2pm arrived at about 7pm and the 4.30 arriving around 10.30pm. Any of these trains would have got Slater and his companion to their destination in time to have a meal before retiring for a full night's sleep. Why then did he choose to travel by the worse possible train along with the newspapers and the milk when there was no apparent pressing reason to do so?

Patrick Nugent was precognoced on January 5, three days after Slater had been arrested in America, and among the questions he was asked was whether he was or ever had been a member of the Sloper Club. As the list of members of the club had by law to be available to the police then in fact the interrogator almost certainly knew the answer before the question was asked. Patrick answered no, which we may take in the circumstances to be the truth. He was then asked the rather obvious follow up question, had he ever been a guest in the club? Again the answer was no but he did conceed that on one occasion he had been outside the Club. On that occasion he had gone to the Club for the purpose of meeting another bookmaker who was a member. However, he had not actually gone into the Club, the interview had taken place in the street outside.

Now the Sloper Club was a private club, indeed that was the only way it could legally operate. Non-members could not just walk in off the street. But guests were permitted provided that their presence was recorded in a special book kept in the entrance hall for that very purpose. It would seem unlikely then that given the hours of opening, from 11pm through to the small hours, that one bookmaker would stand on a winter's night in the street talking to another bookmaker when they could have conversed much more comfortably by stepping inside.

The reason for these questions were quite straight forward, the only direct link the police had so far been able to establish between Slater and Marion Gilchrist was the Sloper Club, and that only tenuously. Slater was a gambler and a member of the Sloper Club while Patrick was also a gambler who had seen and handled Miss Gilchrist's jewellery and who might just conceivably be a regular visitor at the Club.

Of course Patrick was lying when he denied ever having been inside the Club. True he was not a member but then the club had only been open for about eight weeks during which time Patrick had a better place to spend the night hours when in Glasgow, Helen's bed. But it probably was his intention to take out membership at a later date and in any case in spite of the rules there was no real difficulty in gaining admission.

Although on paper an apparently democratic institution where all members were equal within its hallowed walls the reality was something different. The membership were quite definitely divided into two tiers. The lower tier, the vast majority, consisted of no-hope punters who seldom had the luxury of two pennies rubbing together in their pockets. The upper tier, the minority, consisted of members of some financial status such as bookmakers, small businessmen and the like. As though to highlight the difference the two tiers even played different card games. The lower tier played a game known to its adherents as 'muckie' while the upper tier played poker. According to one of the members Slater was, not surprising, a poker player. On the odd occasion that Patrick was undoubtedly present then he too would have been found among the poker players.

The suspicion harboured by the police that Patrick knew Slater was probably correct and, as we shall see shortly, they certainly seemed to act as though their assumption was correct. Indeed it is not to stretch the imagination too far to speculate on whether Slater had tried on an occasion to sell Patrick the brooch he was so desperate to get rid of. After all he had tried to sell it to everybody else who looked as though they might have the money to buy it. Thus the possible connection might well have gone deeper than the police themselves suspected.

The police also suspected that Helen might have known Slater, a suspicion which, given the general circumstances, was really rather remarkable. Indeed the suspicion seems to have been even deeper for at every tributnal before which she appeared the same question was always put. But if Helen did actually know Slater then it could not have been in direct connection with the Sloper Club. One of the few rules seemingly enforced by the organisers of the Club was the rule which rigorously excluded females from Club premises. It follows then that if Helen actually did on some occasion meet Slater then the meeting could only have taken place somewhere away from the Club and almost certainly in the company of Patrick.

Thus by asking the question the police were in fact conceeding that they disbelieved Patrick's claims not to have frequented the Sloper Club. As any such meeting could only have taken place after the beginning of November then the police were also conceding that in spite of his marriage the affair between Helen and Patrick had not ceased with the ringing of the wedding bells.

The police of course had a powerful reason for wishing to establish a connection either between Slater and Helen or failing that between Slater and Patrick. Whoever had killed Marion Gilchrist not only knew about the fortune in jewellery she had in the house but also had some knowledge of the internal layout of the flat and where the jewellery was kept. If they could establish a connection with either Helen or Patrick then this would be a more convincing story than that which had Slater hanging about the street at all hours during the day and night.

The police were hopelessly wrong of course for as we now know Slater had absolutely nothing to do with either the murder or the theft. It follows then that any connection they might have been able to establish could only have been entirely innocent. But this is not to say that the connection did not exist. From November right up until the night of the murder Patrick and Helen were meeting regularly and visiting the various centres of entertainment in the city and Hugh Cammeron tells us that during the same period he and Slater were likewise engaged on practically every single night. It is not then beyond the bounds of possibility that their paths crossed and that Patrick pointed out Slater to Helen as being an interesting character who earned his money dealing in allegedly dodgy jewellery and human flesh.

Chance had thrown Alexander Birrell in Helen's path and she had seized that chance to frame him. Helen was a realist, as a hare Alexander could not be be expected to last the course and so it would do no harm to have another suspect at hand ready for the moment that Alexander's usefulness ceased.

CHAPTER 30

The case against Alexander Birrell, according to the police, collapsed some time late on the Wednesday after the murder when Mary Barrowman came forward as a witness. It was her alleged description of the stranger in the hall which finally put paid to any suspicions the police might still have had against Alexander. This, however, is only a part truth, for the person who had really sunk the case against Alexander had not been Mary but Rowena Liddell.

On the Wednesday afternoon Rowena had gone to the police on her own volition and had made a statement about what she had seen when she had arrived at her mother's house at a few minutes before seven o'clock on the Monday night. Rowena, as we know, had been able to provide a fairly good description of the man. It was she who first told the police about the twisted nose or, as she put it, "a nose you would not see in thousands".

After the conviction of Slater the police disbursed the reward of £200 which had been offered on the basis of the importance of the evidence given by certain of the witnesses, Mary, on the strength of her alleged desription, was given the lion's share, £100, but Mary, on the admission of the police themselves, was not interviewed that Wednesday until after she had finished work at 8pm and the interview took place even later than this. Thus by the time that Mary was interviewed the police already had notice of the misshapen nose and if Mary herself is to be believed it was they who told her what like the man looked.

With Rowena's description at hand the police automatically turned once more to their other two eye-witnesses, Helen and Arthur, to see if they agreed with Rowena's description. Arthur was ambivalent while Helen was still claiming at this point that she had not been able to get a good look at the stranger in the hall. The real test of Rowena's description, however, is to be found not in Helen's denial but in her reaction to it, the description fitted Patrick to a tee. When I was preparing this book I interviewed an elderly gentleman who knew Patrick well and I offered him Rowena's description without revealing the source. He had no difficulty in recognising Patrick. That night, the moment that the police left, Helen suddenly returned to Holytown and Patrick.

It would seem that either later that night or perhaps the following morning the police tried to interview Helen for a second time—she had been staying with an aunt in Glasgow since the murder—and they were not too pleased to dicover that she had disappeared without saying where she was going. She had quite deliberately not told her aunt of her intentions. In the event they did not finally catch up with her again until later that afternoon at the funeral of her mistress. Helen excused her disappearance by saying that she had been so upset at the thought of the funeral that she had gone home to be comforted by her mother. This must have come as something of a surprise for Helen does not seem to have really liked her parents much and that is the only reference she ever makes to them.

The decision to return to Holytown in order to contact Patrick is an indication of the panic she was in. Even if the police had not told her so, and the police did admit that from the Wednesday afternoon they lost all further interest in Alexander, Helen was bright enough to realise that with Rowena's description Alexander was off the hook. The time had come to throw the police another suspect.

The moment that Helen had clapped eyes on Slater she had marked him down as being of some possible future use to her plan, he and Patrick were similar in age, build and colouring, the only marked difference being the shape of the nose. What is more it was common knowledge that it was Slater's intention to leave the country for America. Originally it had probably been Helen's hope that Alexander would have lasted a little longer as a suspect, long enough for

Slater to have left. But events had moved too fast and so it became of importance to find out as quickly as possible what precisely Slater's intentions about leaving were. After all for all that Helen knew he might already have left. The only way they could find out would be for Patrick to head for Glasgow and the Sloper Club.

Witnesses are often more useful for what they leave out than for what they say. One such witness was Alan McLean who told Superintendent Ord where Slater lived. According to McLean, who was a member of the Sloper Club, he found himself walking home one night some distance behind Slater and another man—McLean's way home would take him past Slater's flat—and he saw the two men enter the close at 69 St Georges Road. On this evidence then he assumed that that was where Slater lived. But no such conclusion could be reasonably drawn unless McLean not only knew Slater's companion but also knew that the other man did not live in St Georges Road.

But the police are usually insatiably curious in such matters, they usually are not satisfied with such a statement that the witness saw A. What they want to know is precisely when the witness saw A. Strangely in this case they apparently did not bother to pursue the matter any further. Again when a witness says that he saw A going into a house with someone they usually think it important enough to enquire as to the identity of the other person. Especially when it is patently obvious that the witness knows the identity of the other person. Strangely enough the police again did not pursue this any further.

McLean made his initial statement to the police on the evening of December 25 but it was not until some days later, actually after Slater had been arrested in America, that he was formally precognoced and by which time all other suspects had been dropped in favour of Slater. I think that the real truth of the matter is that when McLean made his original statement he did identify both the night of the incident and the other person who was along with Slater at the time. I believe that the sighting occured in the early hours of the Thursday morning and that the other person was Patrick Nugent.

To establish a contact with Slater was ridiculously easy. The man was a pimp and to gain access to his company all that one had to do was to present himself as a prospective customer. This is what Patrick did and while walking chummily towards St Georges Road he could with little difficulty find out when Slater intended to leave Scotland for America.

Helen was asked a number of times whether she had ever been in Slater's flat as a visitor, an unlikely event given the purpose for which the flat was used and the fact that *Mrs Slater* was a working girl. On the other hand precisely because the flat was used as a brothel Patrick might well have been in the flat and yet he was never asked the question. There is a golden rule among the police and lawyers and that is never to ask a question when you know that the answer will be damaging to your case. Patrick probably quite freely admitted to having been in Slater's flat and to having been in bed with his woman. He probably also at the same time admitted that he had discussed with Slater his proposed departure for America less than 48 hours before this journey began. That would be a good reason for the police to keep such a statement off the record.

The question of course will be asked, why then when Patrick Nugent's name was mentioned in connection with Helen did Slater not realise that Patrick had been the man who had been in his flat as a client. The answer is simple, it is doubtful whether Slater ever knew the names of the clients and in any case Patrick was not generally known by that name. Like so many other Irish men Patrick was known better by the name Paddy.

Patrick and Helen now knew that it was Slater's intention to travel to Liverpool on Friday and if Slater did not reveal the the time of the train he meant to travel by then that was no real problem. Most people in those days carried that invaluable little book, Murray's Diary, a time-table for all the public transport systems in and around Glasgow. By reference to the diary it could easily be figured out that the best train would be the one leaving at 2pm. In fact it was Slater's intention to travel by the 2pm for he had business still to transact that morning but that is another story which I will come to shortly.

Guessing or knowing that Slater intended to travel by the 2pm now presented Helen and Patrick with something of a problem. How should they tell the police? The obvious method, the anonymous letter, while carrying less risk had one drawback, delivery within the city was either early in the morning or at about noon. The police then would be in receipt of the information in plenty of time to apprehend Slater before he left, which would reduce to some extent the idea of his fleeing from justice. But this is only speculation for the method which was used was the messenger.

Lawrence Connolly was a gambler and a member of the Sloper Club who lived in the village of New Stevenson, about a mile from the village of Carfin, which made him almost a neighbour of Patrick. Certainly the two men would have known each other.

The person who actually carried the message to the police was Allan McLean but he makes it perfectly plain that neither the context nor the idea had been his. He says that it was suggested to him by another member of the club that he should go along to the police station and tell the police about a German-Jew who had been trying to sell a brooch which was suspiciously like the one believed to have been stolen from the murdered woman.

One would imagine that Superintendent Ord on being faced by a messenger who was supplying him with important information on behalf of another would have inquired as to the identity of this public spirited if somewhat bashful citizen but if he did, and all the signs are that he did so, then no mention is made of it in the precognition taken later from McLean. There is a note, however, appended to McLean's precognition which states that the police had been endeavouring to contact a man called Lawrence Connolly but without success. The juxtaposition then of the note with McLean's precognition is therefore capable of only one interpretation and that is that the man who sent McLean to the police was Lawrence Connelly.

I think that it is fair to assume that Patrick approached Connolly originally to carry the message. He probably told him some kind of cock and bull story of wanting to get his own back on Slater for some alleged wrong that he had suffered. It is possible also that Connolly owed Patrick some kind of favour for he obviously agreed to do it. But in reflection quite clearly Connolly decided, as well he might, that the whole caper was too dicey to become directly involved in so he in turn turned to Allan McLean, a man who was undoubtedly already known to the police as an informer.

I am firmly of the belief that when Connolly entered into the plot he did so without being aware of the fact that it was no joke but a deadly serious attempt to frame Slater. It must have come as something of a shock then when on the following day he learned of the manhunt for Slater which was filling the papers. Connolly would know only too well that McLean would have given his name to the police and that the police were probably already looking for him. In the circumstances he did the only thing that he could do, he went into hiding. The next week, according to the note on McLean's precognition, on January 1, Connolly sailed from Southampton to South Africa. As it would have cost too much to pursue him the police regretfully wrote him out of the case.

I think that it is fair to suggest that it was Patrick who financed Connolly's hurried departure.

Just about at the same time as the 2pm train from

Glasgow to Liverpool was pulling into Lime Street at the completion of its journey McLean walked into the police station The story he had to tell Superintendent Ord was remarkable for its lack of any substance. He did not personally know Slater in spite of his membership of the Sloper Club. McLean of course was a 'muckie' player. He had never in his life spoken to Slater and indeed he did not even know his name. He thought it was Oscar. As a consequence of his not knowing Slater then his information about the brooch was merely hearsay. He also told Ord that Slater had not been seen in the club on any of the nights following the murder which was most certainly not true for he had been there on at least the Monday, the Tuesday and Wednesday nights. But perhaps most remarkable of all is his claim to have recognised Slater from the description published in all the evening newspapers of that afternoon. In fact there were the descriptions of two men given in the papers which would suggest that McLean could not read.

Had things gone the way that was intended then at the very time that Slater was alighting from the train at Liverpool McLean would have been entering the police station but what no one could have foreseen was that a hitch would develop in Slater's travel plans. The flat and the furniture were to be transferred to two girls who had come up from London on the Thursday to take over. Clearly it was Slater's intention not to travel until the afternoon—most likely by the 2pm train—for there was money involved in the transfer and it would be unlikely that all the affairs would be settled in time for him to catch one of the morning trains. Nevertheless it was Slater's intention that no time should be wasted and so before she had had her breakfast Catherine Schmaltz, the maid, was dispatched by Slater to the hotel where the two girls were staying to bring them to the flat.

Alas for poor Oscar's plans Catherine Schmaltz returned alone. The two girls, who by all accounts were a right pair of hustlers, had no sooner arrived in

Glasgow the previous evening than they immediately started to work. Thus after a long night the two girls were in no condition to rise when the maid called and so poor Catherine had to suffer her master's wrath for the unavoidable failure of her mission. In the event it was not until late in the afternoon before the two girls entered an appearance, too late even to catch the afternoon trains. We may judge the lateness of their arrival by the fact that it was nearly six o'clock in the evening before Slater could get to the station in order to hire a porter.

The significance of this delay is that no one outside the immediate circle of those concerned could have any idea that Slater's travel plans had been changed.

That the record of the statement made Allan McLean to Superintendent Ord some time after 6.30 on the evening of December 25 is incomplete is beyond argument. All mention of Lawrence Connolly has been erased and if one part has been left out then it is a fair assumption that other parts have also been left out.

One of these parts is undoubtedly the fact that Allan McLean told Ord that Slater had already left the city earlier that day. This is the only possible explanation for Powell going to 69 St Georges Road and making no attempt to interview Slater., If Powell already thought that Slater had left then it would have been a waste of time knocking on his door. It would also explain why later, when it was discovered that Slater in fact had not already left, that no action was taken against Powell. As Ord at that moment would have no idea as to the reason for the delayed departure he put it down to an attempt by Slater to cover up his tracks.

McLean also told Ord something else which might had been his own idea, he told Ord that Slater's destination was first London and then the continent. This last piece of information coupled with the last minute switch in departure time by Slater must have seemed to be proof-positive to Ord that he was after the right man. The rest is history.

POSTCRIPT

When I was preparing this book I was able, through the good offices of the Motherwell Times, to get into contact with a small number of people who knew either Helen or Patrick and in one case both. Perhaps not surprisingly none were prepared to permit their names to be published. The villages of Carfin and Holytown are still close-knit communities where one still does not talk about the affairs of an neighbour to strangers, even after eighty years.

After the excitement had died down Patrick, or as he was better known, Paddy Nugent, settled down to become a family man. For a while he continued with his bookmaking business but later he became the owner of a dogtrack in Motherwell. It is interesting to note that Oscar Slater's son by his first marriage also became a bookmaker and was something of a celebrity at the various dogtracks in and about Glasgow. As the dog racing community was never that large then it is impossible that they never met.

Strangely the depth of Paddy's association with Helen was never fully realised even by those who knew him. This in spite of the fact that his name had been mentioned on several occasions in the open court and had duely been reported in the newspapers. One of my informants, an elderly man who lived most of his life in Carfin and who knew Paddy well, was amazed when I told him of the affair between Paddy and Helen, he thought that they were just friends.

A pillar of his church and possessed of a good singing voice Paddy was always to be found at the various services that the Catholic Church is famous for in Carfin. In late life he acquired a reputation for philantrophy in the district and of generosity to his church. To the end, however, he apparently maintained an uncharacteristic emnity towards anyone with the name of Gillon. He died in the late forties having lived for eighty or more years.

Helen's later life is something more of a mystery. After the trial it would appear that she had some difficulty in finding further employment as a maid which is hardly surprising given the publicity she had received. An added factor, however, must have been that the only person available to give her a reference was Margaret Birrell, something that was extremely unlikely after she had tried to frame Alexander. But in any case few employers would wish to have as a maid someone who had been so closely connected with a brutal murder.

After the trial Helen returned to Holytown where she married a miner called Gillon, a marriage which seems to have surprised many who knew her. Apparently Gillon could not be described as the catch of the season. To make matters even more mysterious it would seem that her husband was a catholic. The reason that Helen gave against marrying Patrick although it might be the case that her husband changed his religion.

The general accepted version of Helen's later life is that following WW1 she and her family emigrated to America and certainly she was living in Peoria, Illinois, in 1928 at the time of the appeal. There is also a newspaper report which places Helen in America in the autumn of 1927 when Slater was released from prison. This report, however, is so lacking in hard evidence, for instance it is not disclosed in which town she was allegedly living, that it does not ring true. Nor does the statement allegedly made by Helen to the journalist read like her words.

The version which I am most inclined to believe is one offered by one of my anonymous correspondents. According to this lady, and all I know of her is that she is female, Helen was still living in Holytown up until a few weeks before the appeal when she suddenly departed for America. The move, however, was not permanent for almost immediately after the appeal she and her family were back living in Holytown. The suggestion is, of course, that the purpose of the trip was to put Helen outwith the jurisdiction of the Scottish

Courts. This trip must have cost a deal of money, certainly more than Helen could have afforded out of a miner's wage. At that time the Scottish coal industry was operating what was called the Quota System and most pits were either working only two or three days a week or were closed. If the story is true then someone else must have met the bill and the likeliest person is Patrick.

Helen and her family lived on in Holytown until after WW2 when Helen, it seems that her husband had died in the interval, went to live with a married daughter, Maisy, in Leeds. It is believed that she died in that city in the early fifties.